Love is
a time of enchantment:
in it all days are fair and all fields
green. Youth is blest by it,
old age made benign: the eyes of love see
roses blooming in December,
and sunshine through rain. Verily
is the time of true-love
a time of enchantment — and
Oh! how eager is woman
to be bewitched!

NURSE VERENA AT WEIRWATER

Working at a nursing home, Nurse Verena Frodesley became increasingly involved with her patients' problems. She didn't believe Melusine Colchard's fears, but when Melusine went home for the weekend and was found drowned in the lake she became a murder suspect herself. She knew it was dangerous to travel to Weirwater to nurse Melusine's step-daughter, but it was the only way to solve the mystery and discover which of the three men in her life meant most to her.

Books by Leslie Lance
in the Ulverscroft Large Print Series:

A SUMMER'S GRACE
RETURN TO KING'S MERE
THE YOUNG CURMUDGEON
SPUN BY THE MOON
THE RETURN OF THE CUCKOO

LESLIE LANCE

◆

NURSE VERENA AT WEIRWATER

Complete and Unabridged

ULVERSCROFT
Leicester

First published in Great Britain in 1970 by
Robert Hale Limited
London

First Large Print Edition
published July 1991

British Library CIP Data

Lance, Leslie
  Nurse Verena at Weirwater. — Large print ed. —
Ulverscroft large print series: romance
I. Title
823.914

ISBN 0–7089–2463–8

Published by
F. A. Thorpe (Publishing) Ltd.
Anstey, Leicestershire

Set by Words & Graphics Ltd.
Anstey, Leicestershire
Printed and bound in Great Britain by
T. J. Press (Padstow) Ltd., Padstow, Cornwall

1

"WATER-LILIES?" I echoed. "Matron, I can't . . . "

"Water-lilies and other aquatic plants. How to make a water garden. Illustrated by colour slides," Matron read from the invitation card she was holding. "It should be interesting. Miss Martina Colchard is reputed to be an expert."

"Melusine told me . . . " I swallowed hard. "Matron, please, I *can't*. I can't even think of water-lilies without feeling sick."

"You must certainly go to the lecture, Nurse. If you are sick, so much the better. You'll get this unfortunate affair out of your system," Hilda Hatherby said calmly.

The shrewd grey eyes behind her gold-rimmed glasses were kinder than her tone. I gazed into them in desperate appeal.

"How can I help blaming myself? If I hadn't talked of water-lilies and told her I wanted some for my flower arrangement, Melusine wouldn't have died."

"You can't hold yourself responsible for

1

a sheer accident — and the fact that Mrs Colchard had never learnt to swim," she answered shortly.

"Was it an accident? Nobody saw what happened," I reminded her. "She didn't want to go home. She hated Weirwater. She was frightened of the house . . . and of her husband."

"You're letting your imagination run away with you, Nurse," Matron said severely. "Melusine Colchard was in a highly nervous condition, but there wasn't any suspicion of her having committed suicide. Her neurosis didn't take that form at all. She was suffering from what is commonly called persecution mania. Her delusions . . . "

"Were they all delusions?" I broke in wildly. "She was convinced that someone was trying to kill her."

"An all too common symptom. If you had been here longer, you would have learnt not to attach any significance to it," she assured me.

"Most of what she said sounded dreadfully plausible. There was this money, which she had inherited from her first husband . . . "

I broke off because I sensed that Matron wasn't listening. She had removed her glasses and was polishing them vigorously. She had closed Melusine's case history and wasn't disposed to re-open it.

Perhaps that was natural. By her own efforts, Hilda Hatherby had started and made a success of The Haven. Failure in any degree was anathema to her ... and she would have to number Melusine Colchard among her few failures, even though Melusine hadn't died here.

"It's a mistake to become emotionally involved with a patient, Nurse. You must have had that dinned into you in your training days," Hilda said judicially.

"Of course, but ... she was so small and frightened and vulnerable. She said she couldn't trust anyone — but she was beginning to trust me. Now ... she's dead. She was drowned in her own lake, while she was picking water-lilies for me. Am I to conduct a party to a lecture on water-lilies, as if nothing had happened?"

To my dismay, my voice was shaking. Matron replaced her glasses and subjected me to a chilly scrutiny.

"You would prefer to cherish a guilt

complex and develop a phobia about water-lilies?" she demanded, with biting sarcasm. "If Mrs Colchard's sister-in-law can brace herself to deliver her lecture, you can certainly attend it."

"I can't," I said again, desperately. "Miss Colchard didn't care two pins about Melusine. She resented her brother marrying a widow. She used to torment Melusine by asking pointed questions about her first husband's death . . . and hinting that Melusine had been responsible for it. He died from an over-dose of pheno-barbitone."

She checked me with an impatient gesture.

"I am well aware of Mrs Colchard's background; with the facts, if not with her distorted interpretation of them," she said tartly. "If you had spent twenty years, instead of three months, working among the mentally disturbed, your sympathies would be less easily aroused. You must try to face facts rather than suppositions."

"The fact that Melusine Colchard is dead . . . and the fact that nobody cares?" I said bitterly.

"You've never met Leigh Colchard or

4

his sister, Martina. Who are you to say whether or not they're grief-stricken?" Matron countered. "The facts are quite simple. Mrs Colchard was highly strung and over imaginative, deeply introspective and finding it difficult to communicate. After an unfortunate miscarriage – her second – she became seriously disturbed. She believed that her husband, who naturally wanted a son and heir, blamed her for not having warned him of that earlier miscarriage and had ceased to love her. He was much concerned about her state of mind, as was their family doctor, your friend, Tobin Badgsworth. Between them, they contrived to persuade her to come to us for treatment."

"Yes, but – "

"Let me finish, please!" she said firmly. "She arrived here in a state of silent resentment. She refused to cooperate. She became increasingly withdrawn until, after having tried every other form of occupational therapy without evoking any response, we induced her to attend your flower arrangement course. You managed to break down her resistance and she began to show a gratifying improvement."

"She wouldn't talk because she was afraid that whatever she said would be used against her. She thought the Colchards wanted to have her certified as insane . . . so that her husband could divorce her. She realized that I wasn't involved in any such conspiracy; that I was a stranger here and had never even seen Weirwater or her relations. Also, that I'd had a shock and lost someone very dear to me, so I could understand," I said in a rush. "She trusted me . . . and I failed her. I knew she didn't want to go home that week-end. I had half promised to look her up there on the Sunday afternoon, when I was off duty."

"Instead, you went for a drive with your old friend, Doctor Badgsworth. You should, of course, have foreseen that, bitterly disappointed by your non-arrival, Mrs Colchard would drown herself, on the pretext of gathering water-lilies for you. Deplorable conduct on your part, Nurse. It's scarcely surprising that you have a guilt complex about it," Hilda said, with a heavy sarcasm which made me flinch.

"Put like that, it does sound absurd," I was obliged to admit. "But . . . if I had gone to Weirwater, Melusine wouldn't have been drowned. If we had gone out in the boat together and it had over-turned, I could have saved her. I'm a good swimmer."

"You're also, so I've heard, an experienced rock-climber, but that didn't enable you to save your aunt from falling."

I gasped. I couldn't speak. I felt as if she had run a sword through my ribs. She smiled grimly.

"That's at the bottom of all this about Melusine Colchard. You persist in holding yourself responsible for your aunt's death. Oh, yes, I know about that! Doctor Badgsworth told me when he sponsored your application to join our staff. He warned me that you were recovering from a traumatic shock, as well as from a badly fractured ankle."

Still, I couldn't speak. I knew how Melusine had felt and why she had taken refuge in silence. There were some wounds which could never be healed; wounds which one shrank from displaying even to compassionate eyes.

Hilda Hatherby's steely grey eyes were anything but compassionate as she surveyed me. There was a derision in them which

7

she would never have permitted herself to show towards a patient.

"Doctor Badgsworth assured me that you were basically well-balanced, or I shouldn't have considered your application," she went on coldly. "He believed that you would find release in helping our patients. He omitted to warn me against your tendency to become emotionally involved with them."

"I haven't any such tendency," I said, stung at last into speech. "Melusine was the only one . . . "

"Is that so? Presumably, she gratified your vanity by opening out to you and keeping everyone else at a distance. You're wallowing now in hurt vanity and self-pity rather than in genuine grief for her untimely death?"

I flinched again. She could certainly hit hard — and she wasn't observing Queensberry rules. I felt my cheeks flaming, but I checked the angry retort which sprang to my lips. I admired and respected Hilda Hatherby. She did sterling work at The Haven. I had seen that for myself. I didn't have to take Tobin's word for it. She had gone out of her way to make me feel at home here — and to feel myself a valued addition to the staff. That she had all along known of the tragedy in my past was a shock, but it emphasized the kindness she had shown me.

"You think I am being brutal," she added dispassionately. "I have reason to be. You're an excellent nurse, and I would rather keep you on the staff than regard you as a potential patient."

"*Oh*!" That shook me so hard that I could almost hear my teeth rattling. "There isn't any danger of that. Honestly, Matron, I have tried to take an objective view. But . . . I can't forget the things Melusine told me. About that gloomy old house and the Colchards. She had a natural aptitude for handling flowers, but she was never allowed to demonstrate it in what should have been her own home. Martina Colchard was intensely possessive over the garden and the glasshouses. She dared Melusine to pick any flowers."

"She does a good deal of showing. She wouldn't appreciate having her prize blooms picked. That she was ever deliberately unkind, I find incredible," Hilda said, a pucker behind her greying eyebrows.

9

"There's frequently jealousy between in-laws. No doubt, Mrs Colchard exaggerated it. You'll have to attend Miss Colchard's lectures, and form your own opinion of her."

I gritted my teeth. So . . . we were back at that vexed issue? I wasn't to be let off the lecture? Any sensitive woman would surely have cancelled it, even if it had been arranged weeks ago. That Martina Colchard was prepared to go through with it, within a week of her sister-in-law's death, seemed to me wantonly callous.

"If it's all open and shut, why was the inquest adjourned?" I asked desperately. "Doesn't that look as if there was something odd about Melusine's death?"

"As there were no eye-witnesses, presumably the police wanted to conduct a thorough investigation. You are partly responsible for that," she told me dryly. "Apparently, when Inspector Gilburn called here, you talked wildly to him."

"Did I? I can't remember now what I said. It was such a shattering shock . . . and he did talk as though it might have been suicide . . . "

"Yes? Well — " She glanced at her

large, old-fashioned gold wrist watch. "Mr Thompkin is calling at half-past seven to discuss his mother's condition and the possibility of taking her home. Any dire forebodings on her account, Nurse?"

"Certainly not." Again, I was stung by her sarcasm. "There's nothing wrong with Mrs Thompkin except a passionate jealousy of her daughter-in-law."

"Precisely. You can use your head, as long as your emotions remain unstirred. Mrs Thompkin is middle-aged, spoilt, demanding, and far from appealing — which may have helped you to see her problems clearly," she said quizzically. "That they're self-imposed, doesn't make them any less genuine. Jealousy and self-pity are prevalent factors in what our patients' relations like to call 'nervous breakdowns.' You might remember that."

"Are you implying that I'm suffering from self-pity?" I flashed.

"You yourself are the best equipped to answer that question, Nurse. Now, I must deal with Mr Thompkin — poor man! He's feeling guilty, too. He fears that his belated marriage has wrecked his mother's health."

I caught the ironical twinkle behind her glasses — and felt myself flushing again. I rose with an attempt at dignity which was marred by my wretched ankle. It had stiffened during this prolonged interview, so that I was compelled to limp to the door.

I closed the door after me with exaggerated care . . . because I was longing to slam it. Confound my ankle! Why couldn't it regain its old suppleness? While it was still liable to let me down, it was hopeless to think of going back to a hospital job. I was stuck here. And lucky to be here at that, I reminded myself. What other niche was there for an S.R.N. who couldn't walk far without evincing a painful limp, and couldn't stand for long? Private cases? After Aunt Elspeth's death, I had felt too bruised and shaken emotionally to face the prospect of living with a family.

Tobin had realized that, when he had visited me in hospital. He had seen that I needed a refuge. Thanks to my aunt, I hadn't been obliged to start working again, as soon as my ankle was out of plaster, but I had yearned for something to occupy my thoughts, to banish that dreadful sense of guilt! I had discovered that The Haven was almost as much a haven to its staff as to its patients. Several of my fellow nurses had had some vital reason for opting out of their respective hospitals.

I was lucky to be here, I reminded myself again, pausing to glance back at the big, skilfully modernized old house as I limped across the smoothly mown lawn to the car-park. Originally, it had been a Manor House. Then it had been converted into an expensive country hotel. Apparently, it had been too isolated, too far from the nearest beaches, golf-courses and fishing to attract a sufficient complement of guests. Hilda Hatherby had bought it for a very reasonable price and turned it into a flourishing nursing-home without spoiling its essential character. There wasn't the remotest suggestion of anything institutional.

Hilda was a shrewd business woman and I had heard that she could be ruthless in eliminating nurses who failed to measure up to her standards. I ought to be thankful that she had elected to give me a severe talking to rather than a curt dismissal. From her point of view, I was behaving badly, but I couldn't shrug my shoulders and forget about Melusine. I had this haunting conviction that there had been something odd as well as tragic about her death in the lake called Weirwater . . .

2

"**N**URSE! Nurse Frodesley..." The plump, expensively garbed Mrs Thompkin rose from a deck-chair at the end of the lawn and came hurrying after me, as I was carefully negotiating the stone steps down to the car-park.

I turned reluctantly — and she clasped her elaborately manicured pale pink hands round my arm.

"Nurse, have you seen my son? He was coming to talk to Matron this evening. I've been watching the car-park, but he hasn't come," she said in a rush. "D'you suppose that wife of his has stopped him? She hates me. She realizes that I can see through her."

"He may have parked in the drive, by the front-door," I said, trying to detach myself. I was in no mood to cope with spoilt, pampered Mrs Thompkin and her problems.

"I told him I would wait here for him.

15

I wanted to speak to him before he saw Matron. I'm worried about him, Nurse. I'm sure that girl doesn't feed him properly," she said unhappily. "I feel it's my duty to go home. To check up on that girl and the way she's treating Vic. You know?"

"Yes. I know. Really, though, Mrs Thompkin, there's not much you can do to help," I said. "Young couples have to shake down together. It's wiser not to interfere."

"Interfere?" She drew her plump figure up indignantly. "You sound like that wife of Vic's. She was forever accusing me of interfering. If she really loved him, she would be grateful for a few hints."

"Young wives like to make their own discoveries. They don't want to be told. Try not to worry, Mrs Thompkin," I answered, divided between exasperation and pity. "Your son is old enough to stand up for himself."

"But . . . he won't. He lets her get away with anything. He's besotted about her . . . and she's such a plain little thing, too. She doesn't know how to dress. As for her cooking, it would make you weep.

16

She had never even heard of Bechamel sauce . . . and Vic loves it."

I had noticed that Mrs Thompkin never referred to her daughter-in-law by name, but always called her 'that girl', or 'that wife of Vic's'. I felt sorry for the girl and even more sorry for 'Vic.' Couldn't this doting mother see what she was doing to her son? Possessiveness could create a veritable hell. Aunt Elspeth's had been a mild manifestation compared with Mrs Thompkin's, but it had erected an impassable barrier between me and Tobin Badgsworth.

"If Vic could persuade her to consult dear Doctor Badgsworth, she might listen to him. He's a born charmer." With one of her swift changes of mood. Mrs Thompkin gave me a roguish smile and a playful poke in the ribs. "You would call him a charmer, wouldn't you, Nurse?"

"My aunt did . . . " I said abstractedly.

I could hear the echo of Aunt Elspeth's crisp, assertive voice in my ears, using that same well-worn phrase.

"My dear Verena, the man's a born charmer. You couldn't hope to hold him. You're a dear good girl, but nobody could call you a beauty. You really must try to be sensible."

Had she been my mother, I might have managed to stand up to her. A daughter wasn't normally hog-tied by a sense of obligation to a mother. Aunt Elspeth, who had adopted me when I had been an orphaned ten-year-old, had been in a privileged position. I hadn't been able to defy Aunt Elspeth . . .

"A special friend of yours, isn't he?" Mrs Thompkin persisted.

"Not now. He used to be . . . "

"Oh? Then, there is some truth in the rumour that he's seeing a lot of that poor Mrs Colchard's daughter? She'll be wealthy now . . . and doctors so often marry money. But . . . you're not exactly penniless. That's a nice car . . . "

"It's a must. I can't walk far, so I'm dependent on my car," I answered . . . then wondered irritably why I should find it necessary to defend my apparent extravagance.

Was it because I couldn't shake off my sense of guilt towards Aunt Elspeth? That I still felt vaguely that I oughtn't to have accepted the legacy she had left

18

me? But I had been her only near relative. That cursed imagination of mine! Hilda Hatherby was right. I was in danger of letting it ride me.

It was fantastic to feel myself responsible for Aunt Elspeth's death. I couldn't have saved her. I had done all I could. When she had had that sudden fall, I had risked my own life to climb down to her. Yes, but if I had gone for help instead, mightn't she have survived her injuries? I ought to have foreseen that I would slip, too, and bring an avalanche of shale down on both of us. In my fear for her, I had made the wrong decision. It had been three hours before the rescue party found us. By then, she had been dead and I, one foot pinioned under the debris, had been almost unconscious.

"I can't believe that you bought this lovely little car out of your salary," Mrs Thompkin said archly. "I suspect you of being a dark horse . . . an heiress in disguise."

"Really?" I gritted my teeth. "There's nothing mysterious about me. I must go now, Mrs Thompkin."

I wrenched the car door open and slid awkwardly across the driver's seat. I still found it difficult to get into or out of a car, but, once behind the wheel, I was all right. Thanks to the special automatic gear-change, I didn't have to use my left foot.

"Why the hurry? A date?" she hinted.

"No date, but I'm off duty now," I reminded her pointedly. "Good night, Mrs Thompkin. You'd better go in or you'll be late for dinner."

"Is it dinner time already? Where can my son be? Surely he can't have forgotten his appointment?"

I had an uneasy feeling that she was about to burst into a flood of tears. I sighed inwardly. That was one of the disadvantages of being a nurse . . . or a doctor. You were never really 'off duty'; could never detach yourself wholly from your patients and their demands.

"I shouldn't wait any longer, if I were you," I said, with what patience I could muster. "This is the staff car-park. Most visitors park in front of the house. Why not go in and ask Sister Fulbech? She'll know whether your son's with Matron or not."

"I don't care for Sister Fulbech. She's a very hard woman. She has never been a mother and she can't understand a mother's feelings. You know how I feel."

"Up to a point, but I'm not a mother, either," I said wearily.

"You will be one day. You're very attractive," she assured me. "I'm sorry if it's true that our dear doctor's attention is straying elsewhere."

I could feel my skin burning as I revved up the engine. With a reproachful glance at me, she stepped back and I headed out of the car-park, into the side drive. What had given her the impression that there was 'something between' me and Tobin? There had been, of course, but that had been years ago, when I had been a student nurse and he had been a young houseman.

Aunt Elspeth had effectively squashed that embryo romance. Tobin had been furious at the time, but more from frustration than because he had been deeply in love with me, I had suspected. He might even have been secretly relieved. He hadn't really been in a position to contemplate marriage and I hadn't yet taken my finals.

After he had left the hospital, we had kept in touch, in a casually friendly fashion. He had been kind and considerate when I had been devastated by the shock of Aunt Elspeth's death. He had found this niche for me. We were good friends . . . but he hadn't suggested that we might be anything more.

Tobin was seeing a lot of Melusine Colchard's daughter? That was certainly news to me. Not daughter, though. Stepdaughter. Melusine had never had a child. That had been one — or perhaps the main — cause of her acute depression. She had been convinced that she had failed her husband — both her husbands. Her stepdaughter was the only child of her first husband. Melusine had scarcely spoken of her. I had gathered the impression that the girl — Reine, wasn't she called? — was a negligible quantity.

Once, Melusine had said: "I don't suppose Reine has ever forgiven me for marrying her father . . . or for his death . . . but she likes her stepfather. In fact, she's much more at home at Weirwater than I am."

Poor Melusine! She seemed to have been conscious all her life of a sense of failure. That had puzzled me, because she had been enchantingly lovely, with her naturally golden hair, enormous blue eyes, and delicately cut features.

In one of her sudden bursts of confidence, she had said: "I'm such a fool. I always do and say the wrong thing. Heaven knows why Leigh married me! I'm all wrong for him. He needed someone competent and energetic; a born countrywoman, like his sister, who could have helped him in the Nurseries. I love flowers but I don't know the first thing about them."

"Men don't usually marry women like their sisters. Probably, you appealed to the romantic streak in him," I had said consolingly.

"Romantic?" She had puckered her ivory forehead. "Leigh isn't romantic. Unless it's romantic to be dedicated to Weirwater and the Colchard reputation for rose growing. Perhaps he is romantic about his roses. Not about people."

"He married you . . . "

"Reine said all along that the money was the attraction." She had sighed dispiritedly. "Harry, Reine's father, left me a lot of money. Martina thinks Leigh married simply in order to have a son to carry on at Weirwater. I ought to have warned him . . . but I'm so stupid. I never guessed . . . "

Heavy, silent sobs had shaken her. I had taken her in my arms as if she had been a child, and she had clung to me, quivering as if in agony.

"Now . . . I can't ever have a baby . . . " she had said brokenly. "I would have tried again, even if it had killed me, but . . . but they operated on me in hospital without even waiting till I was conscious and they could ask me."

"Your husband must have given his consent."

"They told him it was to save my life. He hadn't any alternative, had he? Leigh isn't a cruel man. He's a brute sometimes, but not cruel. It's just that he doesn't understand . . . and I can't talk to him. He listens to Martina . . . and she hates me. She would have been glad if I had died. She would like to kill me."

I had thought she was exaggerating, but I hadn't dared to say so. At the least hint that I found her revelations incredible, Melusine had withdrawn into her silent brooding again. I had never discovered how she really felt about her husband.

I couldn't guess whether she still loved him — or had ever loved him. I had never heard her use the word 'love', in connection with anyone.

She had 'loved' flowers. She had 'loved' my flower arrangements. She had 'loved' my car, in which I had occasionally taken her for a drive in my off duty periods. She had 'loved' pretty clothes and sweet things, in a child-like fashion, without any discrimination. Once I had bought her a filmy blue nylon head-scarf from Woolworths because it had been the exact blue of her lovely eyes. She had been as delighted with that scarf as if it had been one of the choicest Jacqmars. She had worn it constantly. She had been wearing it when her sister-in-law had fetched her for that last, fateful week-end. Perhaps it had been covering her bright hair when she had over-balanced and fallen into the lake . . .

I tried to check my imagination there. It was futile to dwell on the irrevocable. Melusine was dead. I could torment myself with this wretched feeling that I had failed her, but I might equally well blame Tobin. It had been he who had dissuaded me from going over to Weirwater last Sunday afternoon.

"It's ten miles away, up the narrowest of narrow lanes, and the Colchards won't thank you for barging in on them. Perhaps our patient won't, either. She may imagine that you're checking up on her," he had reasoned.

"She *asked* me to look in if I could," I had protested.

"Well, you can't. You're coming up on the moors, with me," Tobin had said decisively. "Heavens, girl! Don't you see enough of your patients when you're on duty? You need some moorland air to blow away the cobwebs."

I had let him over-rule me. I hadn't really wanted to present myself at Weirwater without an invitation from Melusine's husband or sister-in-law. I had told myself that Melusine would have to come to terms with her husband. She could scarcely stay on at The Haven indefinitely.

She had made a good recovery physically from the shock of her miscarriage and hysterectomy. In the last few weeks, except for occasional fits of brooding, she had seemed normal enough, mentally, too.

Indeed, I couldn't see that she had ever been mentally sick. Her troubles had seemed to me wholly emotional.

That, was true of most of our patients. The Haven had, so Sister Fulbech, who had been with Hilda Hatherby from its inauguration, had told me, been started as a Maternity Home. It still had a heavily booked up Maternity Wing for well-to-do private cases. It had been Doctor Hurst Green, Tobin's senior partner and a specialist in nervous disorders, who had induced Hilda to launch out on the therapeutic side — for those who were physically and/or mentally disabled. People who had incurred some physical disability needed time and the right surroundings in which to learn to adapt themselves, he had explained. It was difficult for them to resume a normal home-life immediately after their discharge from hospital. Those who had lost a limb had to be helped to adjust themselves to the drawbacks of an artificial substitute. Partial paralysis came into the same category. Too sudden a transition from hospital to home could have a disastrous effect. It was a valuable and vital job to restore a crippled person's equilibrium and help her to regain a measure of independence.

'Rehabilitation' was a clumsy, unendearing word but Tobin had contrived to fire me with his own enthusiasm – and Doctor Hurst Green's – for the process. I had needed a bit of it, myself, although I had been assured that my ankle would become virtually normal again in time. My limp, which would have been a serious disadvantage in most places, was actually something of an asset here. It convinced the disabled that I could sympathize with their problems.

The Haven was well named. The little country town of Ashley Combe might equally well have been called 'The Haven,' I thought, as I drove up the narrow, old-fashioned Fore Street. It wasn't even a market town. It was a complete backwater. According to Sister Fulbech, it had scarcely changed at all in the last twenty years. It was odd to reflect that it was only a few miles from the congested A38 and its constant stream of traffic. Ashley Combe wasn't 'on the way to' anywhere, so, even in the height of the holiday season, very few tourists discovered it, and there was virtually no demand for 'bed and breakfast.' There was never any problem about finding suitable accommodation for those members of Hilda Hatherby's staff who elected to 'live out'.

Even so, I had been exceptionally fortunate in my rooms and in my landlady. She was the widow of a former local schoolmaster; a pleasant, cheerful little woman and an excellent cook. Her one drawback, from some people's point of view, was her fondness for cats. She had nominally half a dozen of her own but she fed any stray which wandered into her orbit. Frequently, the strays attached themselves to her. Luckily, I liked cats and had no strong feelings about finding a cat on my bed or in my favourite armchair. That appeared to endear me to Mrs Nocton and she looked after me as if I were a prize winning Persian.

Ashley Combe lay in a secluded, wooded valley, quite close to Dartmoor, but away from the main roads to the Moor. Mrs Nocton's cottage was up a side lane. Its pleasant, rambling garden backed on to the woods . . . a fact which the cats appeared to appreciate but the owner of the said woods

29

didn't. Mrs Nocton lived in fear that one of the cats would meet an untimely end at the hands — or the gun — of the gamekeeper. She tried to get them in at night, but some of them were born hunters and managed to elude the curfew.

I turned into the quiet, tree bordered lane — and recognized the car outside Mrs Nocton's gate with an involuntary flicker of my brows. Mrs Nocton had no close neighbours and wasn't a gossip, but it was rare for Tobin to call at the cottage. He had acquired discretion in the years he had spent with Doctor Hurst Green.

As I drew up behind his sleek white Rover, he sprang out and came up to my window, frowning.

"You're very late this evening, Verena," he said abruptly. "Anything wrong?"

"No. Matron summoned me for a heart to heart when I came off duty, and then I had some difficulty in getting away from Mrs Thompkin. I wasn't expecting you . . . "

"I've been waiting forty minutes."

"I'm sorry," I said, puzzled by the unfamiliar jerkiness of his tone. "I couldn't have known that, could I? Why didn't you go into the cottage?"

"Among all those cats? No, thank you!" but his grimace was abstracted and he was glancing up the lane in an apprehensive fashion. "You haven't seen Gilburn yet?"

"Gilburn?" I echoed blankly. "Who's Gilburn? Oh! That policeman? Why should I have seen him?"

"He told me he was going to interview you again. I had to warn you."

"Warn me? Of what?"

"To be careful how you answer his questions. I've an uneasy suspicion that he has it in for you."

"For *me*?" I said incredulously. "What am I supposed to have done? I haven't been exceeding the speed limit or parking on the wrong side of the road."

"Gilburn doesn't deal with traffic offences. He's plain clothes. It's about this Colchard affair," Tobin said, swiftly and unsmilingly. "Something — or someone — has put it into his head that you're involved."

"Involved? But . . . I told him all I could when he called at The Haven."

"He doesn't appear to think so."

He paused, looking so concerned that I blinked at him.

Tobin was quite the most handsome man I had ever encountered. At St. Wilbraham's, my training hospital, impressionable students had been wont to declare that 'it isn't fair. No young doctor should be that good-looking . . . and brilliant as well. He's a born heartbreaker.'

He was tall and slim and very dark, with near-black hair and eyes and a warmly olive skin. All his features were finely and firmly moulded, and his figure had the natural grace of an athlete. I had heard him compared tritely to a 'Greek god' and a 'Spanish grandee.' In actual fact, he was Cornish by birth and pure Celt on both sides.

In his prep school days, he had been nicknamed 'Badger,' and the name had stuck. It was more appropriate than the 'Toby', used by his family. There was a badger-like determination and purposefulness about him.

"I don't understand," I said, with a faint quiver of apprehension — as if his obvious uneasiness were contagious. "What information does the Inspector imagine I possess?"

"I wish I knew! For some reason, he

has been checking up on you thoroughly. You'd better not try to keep anything from him."

"Anything? What?" I asked in bewilderment.

He hesitated again, then said in a rush: "About your aunt. He catechized me about you this morning. It was no use trying to parry his questions. He knew too much."

I shook my head dazedly.

"Too much? But . . . what is there to know? And . . . what has my past history to do with Melusine?"

"Nothing. He has just got this fantastic idea into his head," Tobin said grimly. "He had the nerve to say it was 'quite a coincidence that Nurse Frodesley should have been involved in two fatal accidents.' He smiled in a nasty way when I reminded him that, at the time of Melusine Colchard's death, we were up on the moors. He asked if I could prove that."

"Good heavens!" I said helplessly. "Then . . . he doesn't think it was an accident? Why not?"

"He's a cagey bird. He did admit that the water-lilies she had been clutching had been placed in her hand after she was dead . . . to suggest accidental death."

"Oh!" I caught my breath sharply. "He thinks Melusine committed suicide and that someone tried to cover it up and make it look like an accident? I'll never believe that. She was so much better. She wouldn't have killed herself, unless . . . "

"What?"

"There could have been a sudden, blazing row. She might have jumped into the lake to frighten her husband. But . . . surely he would have gone in after her? She couldn't swim."

"She could have waded ashore. The lake is deep in the middle but not round the verge. She went in from a boat," Tobin said shortly.

"Not deliberately."

"You'd better not insist on that. If we rule out accident and suicide, what's the alternative?"

"Murder," I said. In a way, it was a relief to have my vague fears flushed from the coverts. "Someone killed her. Then, she wasn't imagining things . . . "

"You take it very coolly . . . but you're not given to hysterics, are you, Verena?" There was an odd note in his tone which made me stare at him in heightened bewilderment. "I was told that, when the search party found you and your aunt, everyone was astonished by your composure."

"I was barely conscious and beyond feeling much. Besides, I knew she was dead. I couldn't reach her, but I heard her die . . . "

"You didn't even cry."

"I don't cry easily . . . and never about things that really hurt. What are you getting at, Badger?" I demanded.

"I wish to hell I knew! There's something about you, Verena . . . a kind of impenetrable fence. I loved you desperately in the old days. I'm still in love with you, come to that, but I'll be hanged if I know what lies behind the fence," he said irritably. "Still waters run deep . . . and can be dangerous."

"Dangerous?" I echoed unbelievingly. "Are you implying that I pushed Aunt Elspeth over that precipice?"

"Did you? No — " as I was about to voice an angry retort. "I don't want to know. If anyone asked for a timely shove, that damn' woman did. She intended to possess you, body and soul. If you had rebelled, I wouldn't blame you."

I couldn't speak. The shock was too great. I could only stare at him. This was the only man I had ever loved . . . and he could think that of me?

In the sudden silence, I heard the sound of a car's slowing and changing gear. Tobin glanced quickly up the lane.

"Damn and blast!" he swore softly. "Here comes Gilburn. I hadn't meant him to catch me here. He'll suspect that we're cooking up something . . ."

"A cast-iron alibi?" I suggested bitterly. "Proof that I didn't go round the bend and push Melusine into the lake?"

"Don't take that tone to Gilburn! This isn't a poor joke. It's serious. The man's gunning for you," Tobin said urgently. "Watch your step!"

"You're being fantastic," I flashed. "I'm not afraid of Inspector Gilburn. I've nothing to hide."

It wasn't an official police car which drew up behind mine. It was a rakish looking, low slung sports car. The man who swung himself out of it didn't look in the least official — or formidable — either.

He was a slight, sparely built man, with mouse-coloured hair, sprinkled with silver, and a neat-featured, inconspicuous kind of face. In a crowd, he would appear negligible and virtually unrecognizable. Possibly, that was an asset to him in his detective work.

"Good evening, Miss Frodesley . . . " His thin lips curved into an automatic smile, but his eyes weren't smiling as he glanced from me to Tobin. "Ah, Doctor Badgsworth! Sorry if I'm interrupting anything, but I would be grateful if I could have a few words with Miss Frodesley."

"Good evening, Inspector! I had just been telling Miss Frodesley that you wanted to see her." Tobin didn't even attempt his usual flashing smile. "I'd better push off now . . . unless you would like me to stay, Verena?"

"Why should you? The Inspector doesn't bite, does he?" I forced a smile. "I'll be seeing you . . . "

"Right! If that's the way you want it — " but Tobin was still frowning as he headed for his Rover.

3

"YOU and Doctor Badgsworth are old friends, Miss Frodesley?" the Inspector observed thoughtfully.

"Since my training days." I felt at a disadvantage, seated behind the driving wheel and talking through the window, so that I had to look up at him. "Exactly how many words do you want, Inspector?"

"How many?"

"If this interview is going to take long, perhaps you would rather come into the house. You might find it easier, for your note-taking," I said, with a glance at the shiny black notebook he had opened. "Is this a case of 'anything you say will be taken down and may be used in evidence'?"

If I had hoped to disconcert him, I failed. He didn't flick an eyelash. He merely smiled.

"Oh, no! This isn't an official visit ... and, at this stage in our inquiries, I don't consider it necessary to give you the official warning," he said easily. "Yes, I dare say we should be more comfortable indoors, where you can put up that stiff ankle. Is it painful?"

"Sometimes. When I've been standing." I had tried hard not to be over-sensitive about my wretched ankle, but I still disliked any conventional sympathy from strangers. I added defiantly: "It's just a temporary inconvenience."

He nodded and opened the car door. As I slid out, he gripped me firmly by the arm.

"Thank you! I can manage," I said, but he kept hold of my arm with one hand and opened the neat white gate with the other.

In the still, warm, September air, I was conscious of his pine-scented after-shave lotion. He had that kind of pale clear skin which always looked as if it had been newly shaved. He was a bit of a dandy, I thought, noting the impeccable cut of his grey lounge suit, and the fresh, uncrumpled look of his white shirt.

"You have comfortable quarters here?" he asked.

"Very. Virtually self-contained. My own

bedroom, bathroom and sitting-room. This way — " as he was about to pilot me to the front door. "There's a garden door leading into my sitting-room. I don't use the front door."

"Very convenient. You can come and go without disturbing your landlady."

"Yes. It's very convenient when I'm on late duty. Though, Mrs Nocton usually hears me and bobs up with a hot drink."

A narrow, flagged path led round the cottage to the garden door. The Inspector helped me up the three shallow steps to the unlocked glass door. Then, to my relief, he relinquished my arm, and I sank thankfully down on my well-sprung, leather covered sofa. He stood motionless for a moment or two, glancing round the room like a cat in strange surroundings.

"Nice. Very nice!" he commented. "You have your own furniture here?"

"Some of it is mine. Would you like a drink — or isn't that permitted? There's sherry on the sideboard."

"I told you, this isn't an official visitation," he repeated. "Sherry would be very acceptable. I've had a long day, and I expect you've been hard at it, too."

He walked over to the handsome carved oak sideboard which had been Aunt Elspeth's. His movements were light and cat-like. He poured out two glasses of Amontillado and brought one over to me, with a conventional little bow.

There was a sudden upheaval among the cushions at the other end of the sofa and Leo, a large orange coloured cat, emerged, yawning and blinking. He stretched gracefully then made a swift leap on to my lap, purring a welcome.

"*Don't!*" I said, as he began to knead me and his claws dug into my stockings. "Quiet, now!"

I tried to induce him to sit down on my lap. He was a very affectionate cat. He rubbed his head against my hand and gazed up at me with adoring amber eyes.

"Yours?" Inspector Gilburn inquired.

"No. A fellow resident."

"You're fond of cats?"

I was aware of his light, hazel eyes, watching me, as I held my glass of sherry out of Leo's reach and sipped it.

"I like most animals," I said flatly. "You're not here to inquire into my personal tastes, I imagine?"

"You would be surprised how often we obtain valuable leads from character and background," he answered blandly. "Are you a good judge of character, Miss Frodesley?"

"About average." I looked at him challengingly. "I don't believe that Melusine Colchard drowned herself — if that's what you have in mind. Doctor Badgsworth told me that you weren't satisfied that her death was due to an accident."

"Her husband isn't. You've met him?"

"No. I don't know any of her family. They didn't visit her at The Haven."

"That, I understand, was by her own wish. In her confused mental condition, she appeared — in the popular phrase — to have 'turned against them.' I believe that's not unusual," he said judicially.

"Confused? Her emotions were certainly confused . . . but her brain wasn't."

"You wouldn't agree that she suffered from delusions?"

"Delusions? Illusions? What are they? Most of us delude ourselves at times, or indulge in illusions," I said impatiently. "Probably, she exaggerated her husband's and sister-in-law's reactions. She was over-sensitive."

"You were her friend and confidante?"

"I tried to be. It was important that she should talk to someone. She was much too withdrawn."

"You took her for drives. To Plymouth and Newton and Torquay."

"With Matron's knowledge and approval. It did her good to get out and have a prowl round the shops. She was like a child in her enjoyment of an outing," I gazed at him perplexedly. "What are you getting at, Inspector?"

"You knew that she was a wealthy woman?"

"She told me that her first husband had left her 'a lot of money'. I don't know what she called 'a lot'. She didn't spend money lavishly when we were out together. I paid for the petrol and the meals we had."

"She gave you presents, no doubt?"

"She gave me one present. That pottery bowl on the sideboard."

"An odd gift," he commented.

"Oh, no! Very appropriate. Perfect for a flower arrangement, featuring water. I suppose it was indirectly responsible for her death," I said, flinching inwardly. "I had planned to do an arrangement in it for the Ashley Combe Flower Show. I thought water-lilies would look well in it. She was going to bring me some, to try the effect."

"Flower arranging is your hobby?" He glanced thoughtfully at the arrangement of dried grasses, bracken, and berries from the hedgerows in the copper bowl on the table. "Unusual at your age . . . but Miss Hatherby told me that it was one of the reasons why she took you on at The Haven. Have you been interested in it for long?"

"It was my aunt's idea. I was orphaned as a child, and my father's only sister adopted me. She was a dedicated botanist and gardener. She specialized in rather rare plants. She liked entering for Flower Shows, but she wasn't artistic, and she wasn't good at staging her entries. She conceived the idea that I should study flower arranging. I went to classes . . . and found them fascinating."

"That was the aunt who was killed so tragically? While you were on a climbing expedition together?"

"Yes. Except that we weren't climbing

for pleasure. We were looking for plants."

He was raising one eyebrow expectantly, but rebellion surged up in me. Why should I relive that ghastly moment — when Aunt Elspeth had leaned over too far, slipped, and fallen headlong — for this detective's benefit? Did he expect me to protest that I couldn't have saved her? I had no proof of that. There hadn't been any eyewitnesses.

"I don't see what this has to do with Melusine Colchard's death," I said.

"Don't you?" he said speculatively. "You're an intelligent woman. Possibly, you're an opportunist, too."

"I didn't ask my aunt to adopt me . . . or to leave me her money. If you're implying that I pushed her over the edge, you're right off target. I didn't. I was fond of her."

"Even though she had broken up your romance with Doctor Badgsworth?"

"Heavens! You have been probing into my affairs." I felt anger rising in me. I fought to keep it under control. "My aunt couldn't have stopped me from marrying Doctor Badgsworth. I was of age."

"Then — "

"She talked me out of it . . . made me see that I owed it to her to complete my training . . . and that Doctor Badgsworth wasn't really in a position to think of marriage." I met his inquiring glance unflinchingly. "What justification have you for these highly personal questions? Why should the police be interested in my past?"

"Officially, we're not. I was merely trying to fill in the background; to get the picture clear," he said mildly. "For my own satisfaction."

"Indeed? Well, I hope you are satisfied."

He didn't answer. He opened his notebook again.

"We're not quite clear about your movements on Sunday afternoon and evening," he observed. "You had arranged to visit Mrs Colchard at Weirwater?"

"It wasn't an arrangement. She asked me to look in, if I could. I wasn't keen on the idea. I didn't know her family. I told you all that."

"Yes. You went up to Dartmoor with Doctor Badgsworth. According to his statement, you wanted to be back here in time to attend Evensong at St Cuthbert's, so he brought you back just before six o'clock. Correct?"

"Yes."

"Oddly enough, nobody remembers having seen you at St Cuthbert's."

"Oh, heavens! Have you been probing into that? What on earth will people think?" I demanded in exasperation. "Why didn't you ask *me*? I could have told you that I didn't go to Evensong after all."

"How was that?"

"Usually I take Mrs Nocton. It's a long walk for her to the church, so she's glad of a lift. Last Sunday, after I'd changed, one of her cats started to have kittens. She decided she had better stay — in case there were complications — but she urged me to go without her."

"Yes?"

"I got out the car and drove towards the town. Then . . . I changed my mind. I was tired and my ankle was aching. Doctor Badgsworth and I had walked up to Hound's Tor . . . "

I paused, recalling the misgivings which had disturbed me last Sunday evening. That outing with Tobin had left me restive and uneasy. Not because of anything he had said, but because of the way he had looked at me and taken my arm to help me over the rough ground. I had known then that, if I wanted to, I could fan the seemingly dead ashes between us into a glowing fire.

"So?" Inspector Gilburn prompted me.

"I didn't go to church. I drove around for a while."

"You drove towards Weirwater."

"Oh, no! At least, not consciously. I don't know exactly where Weirwater is."

"The nearest village is South Tapwick. I understand that you stopped for petrol there."

"I did stop for petrol. I didn't notice the name of the garage — or the village. I'm a stranger in this part of the world."

"You have a car."

"But not a great deal of time and energy to spare for exploring the countryside. I didn't go to Weirwater on Sunday evening — or on any other occasion!" I said irritably. "I wish I had gone to see Melusine . . . but I suppose she was dead when I reached South Tapwick — "

"There is some doubt about the time of her death. Between five and seven is the nearest we can get to it on the medical evidence," he said evenly. "According to

48

the petrol pump attendant, he filled your tank just before seven-thirty, when he went home. He remembered your car. A black Swallowtail with a broad red line around it. Not a common sight."

"Possibly unique," I agreed bitterly. "My aunt had that red line painted on — to make the car easy to spot in a car-park. So — what? Are you suggesting that I went to Weirwater and pushed Melusine into the lake? You must be crazy — as crazy as I would have been if such a project had ever entered my head."

"Crazy? Killers have their own logic. Where they differ from the rest of us in their sense of values."

I blinked at him. He looked — and sounded — entirely serious.

"You are suspecting me," I said incredulously.

He shook his head.

"I'm reserving judgement. In my job, when one is investigating a possible crime, one has to consider means, opportunity, and motive. The means were simple."

"Except that I could scarcely have overturned a boat and swum ashore without soaking my clothes."

"A resourceful young woman would have taken a change of clothing with her."

"Oh, nonsense! Nobody could be that cold-blooded," I flared. "Even supposing I was somewhere in the vicinity, what possible motive could I have had for drowning Melusine? I was fond of her."

"You were, you told me, fond of your aunt . . . but she died in a tragic accident . . . and you benefited financially from her death," he reminded me ruthlessly.

"Hell! This is beyond a joke." I clenched my hands tightly together. "You've said more than enough, Inspector. I've tried to keep my temper, but you've gone too far now. You'd better scram before I hurl something at you."

"As you please," he said calmly. "You've certainly kept your temper remarkably well. You have considerable powers of self-control."

"A nurse needs to have. Is that another score against me? Should I have refused to answer your impertinent questions?"

He shrugged his slender shoulders and rose, but he didn't head for the door. He paused, looking down at me with the same kind of frown which Tobin had worn when he had stood beside my car window. 'Still waters run deep,' indeed? Was that trite adage in the Inspector's mind, too? Neither he nor Tobin had been brought up by Aunt Elspeth, with her aversion to any display of emotion.

"It's difficult to be tactful in a case like this," the Inspector said reflectively. "I should get a severe tick-off from my superiors if they knew I had come here, unofficially."

"Then, why did you come?"

"My curiosity was aroused . . . and I'm only human. I find your personality definitely intriguing."

"Thank you! If my brain worked as you appear to imagine, I should be a suitable candidate for the Chamber of Horrors," I said. "A nurse who goes around eliminating her patients for no known motive must certainly possess an 'intriguing personality'."

"No known motive?" he echoed. "Am I to believe that the motive is unknown to you?"

"Certainly. I mean, there simply isn't any motive. Are you imagining now that I'm in love with Melusine's husband — whom

I've never even met?"

"Oh, no! I was thinking of the money. Are you unaware that she had made a new Will, leaving the bulk of her estate to you?"

"Leaving me money?" I felt as though the floor had given way beneath my feet. "That's not possible. When could she have made a new Will?"

"When you took her into Plymouth, a fortnight ago."

"No! I don't believe it. She didn't have a chance. Besides, why should she do anything so extraordinary?"

He didn't answer. He just stood there, his light hazel eyes raking my face.

"Hell!" I said, my wits beginning to work again. "We went to a Salon to have our hair washed and set. When I emerged from my cubicle, Melusine was in the waiting-room, with her hair untouched. She said she had suddenly felt faint and couldn't face the drier. I didn't think anything of it, except that perhaps I had let her do too much that morning. You mean that she slipped out and went to a strange solicitor? Without telling me a word about it?"

He shrugged his shoulders again. "Was that how it happened?"

"How can I know?" I countered. "It doesn't make sense. Why would she do such a thing?"

"You can probably answer that more convincingly than I can," he said dryly.

"Because she was afraid of her husband? She really did think that he wanted to get rid of her?" I said confusedly. "She meant to safeguard herself? And − and − it didn't work. She's dead. She died before she'd brought herself to tell him she'd made a new Will? Then . . . he did kill her. Oh, how horrible! If only she hadn't been so secretive . . . "

"I understood that she had confided in you."

"In fits and starts. Not to that extent," I said dully. "I didn't realize that she believed herself to be in actual physical danger. He could have asked her to give him a divorce . . . if he was all that set on having a son and heir. He didn't have to kill her."

"Precisely. There is no reason to suppose that Leigh Colchard had any hand in his wife's death," the Inspector said in mild reproof. "His story is that he spent the evening lifting roses in preparation for a Horticultural Show. He had tea with his wife and left her sitting in a deckchair on the terrace. At eight o'clock, his sister called him to supper. It was discovered then that Mrs Colchard was missing."

"But . . . someone must have seen her between tea and supper time."

"Miss Colchard was out, picking blackberries. Miss Elland was in the house, in the bathroom, washing her hair and experimenting with a colour rinse."

"They all just went off and left Melusine alone?" I said incredulously. "When it was her first weekend at home for months? What kind of family is that?"

"Miss Colchard said frankly that there had been an argument at tea-time; that she had lost patience with her sister-in-law and told her that a mental home was the obvious place for her. She added that she might have provided an incentive for suicide by her plain speaking."

"But . . . it wasn't suicide." I tried to brace myself; to think clearly. "Someone is lying, of course. Someone knows exactly what happened."

"Someone . . . " he repeated.

"And you believe I'm that someone? That I'm some kind of monster, going around murdering people for money?"

To my amazement, his thin features were illuminated by a sudden smile; a smile of genuine amusement.

"No, Miss Frodesley. I don't see you as a monster, but as a very attractive and intelligent woman. Too attractive for my peace of mind — which is why I've been sticking my neck out on your account this evening," he said. "Like our mutual friend, Doctor Badgsworth . . . "

"I don't understand . . . "

"Don't you? Before long you will. Once this sort of investigation gets under way, it's equivalent to having a searchlight focused on everyone who is even remotely connected with the victim. I have, in my clumsy way, been endeavouring to prepare you for it."

"Very kind of you! I've a feeling that you should have been a Q.C. rather than a detective."

I didn't know what made me voice that thought as it sprang to my mind, but he started slightly.

"That's uncommonly perceptive of you. It was my first ambition, but I had to abandon it from lack of means." Again, unexpectedly, he smiled. "I, too, received a handsome legacy — after the death of a godmother whom I scarcely knew — but it was too late, then."

"Bad luck for you, but good luck for some people. You would have raked hostile witnesses mercilessly."

"My one objective is always to uncover the truth."

"Then, I hope you succeed in this case," I said feelingly.

"It may take quite a time, but I shall," he said — and I wasn't sure whether he intended that as a promise or a warning. "Thank you for the sherry — and your patience — Miss Frodesley. Good-bye for the present."

4

BEFORE I could remove Leo, now peacefully snoozing on my lap, and rise, Inspector Gilburn had let himself out of the glass door. I had a glimpse of his slim, elegantly clad back as he took the path round the house. Then he was out of sight. I listened automatically for the sound of the sports car's engine . . . but there was only silence.

Evidently, he was subjecting my landlady to an interrogation about my movements.

I reached for my handbag, and got out my cigarette case. I didn't smoke much, but I felt the need of a stimulant now. I lit up and leaned back against the cushions, conscious that I was badly shaken. Almost as shaken by the man Gilburn as by the detective. 'An intriguing personality?' That phrase was certainly applicable to *him*. He was a long way removed from the run of the mill policeman who had interviewed me after my aunt's death.

Such an apparently inconspicuous,

ordinary looking man, apart from his clothes and sports car — and all the more dangerous on that account. It hadn't taken me many minutes to appreciate that he had both brains and breeding. He should have been a barrister, rather than a member of a country C.I.D. What was he doing in Ashley Combe? Had he, like myself, had some compelling reason for seeking a refuge here? If he was in the habit of 'sticking his neck out,' as he had termed it, perhaps, in some larger Force, he had had the chopper applied by his superior officers.

A mistake on their part. Gilburn was clever and deserved more scope. He had handled me skilfully, provoking me into speech when, in the normal way, I should have remained silent. He had got under my guard . . . and that was an achievement. In the four years since I had parted from Tobin, I had sought to make myself man-proof. No more heart flutterings or heart burnings for me, I had vowed. Yet, now I had been shown that I wasn't immune as I had hoped.

On Sunday evening, I had been wondering if I had been wise to venture within

Tobin's orbit again. I had been certain, when he had suggested The Haven, that we had outgrown what my aunt had called 'that boy and girl romantic nonsense.' On Sunday, I had sensed that Tobin had retained a lingering tendresse for me. This evening, I had seen it even more clearly. He had been genuinely het up about me. Obviously, he believed that I had come here on his account.

The unconscious vanity of men! Tobin really did suspect that I had given Aunt Elspeth a fatal shove for his sweet sake; either in revenge because she had parted us, or else because I had yearned for the freedom to contact him again. How could he think me capable of such an action and still care about me? Perhaps, like the Inspector, he saw me as an 'opportunist.'

I ought to know how to cope with Tobin, but Gilburn was in a different category. Gilburn hadn't been trying to disarm me, when he had admitted that he found me attractive and intelligent. That had been the moment of truth. He was afraid that I was involved in Melusine's death. If there was an intensive investigation, presumably he would be in charge of it — and in duty bound to report his findings. He wanted to get at the truth, but he didn't want it to lead to me.

He had given me some nasty shocks. Yet, he had left me with a sense of relief rather than of apprehension. I was fiercely glad that Melusine's death wasn't to be written off as an accident. I need not now torment myself with remorse. She hadn't died because she had been gathering water-lilies for me. She had died because someone had wanted her dead.

Someone? Who? On the face of it, Leigh Colchard was the obvious answer. Just a shade too obvious, perhaps? When a wealthy young wife died mysteriously, wasn't her husband bound to be the first and main suspect? Leigh Colchard must have seen that. Had he hoped that he could make it appear a tragic accident?

Had it been his hands which had clasped Melusine's dead hand around a bunch of water-lilies? Whoever had done that must be essentially cold-blooded. Conventionally minded, too. It would surely have been easier to have faked a suicide? It wasn't unusual for patients in 'a disturbed condition' to commit suicide. Neither Tobin, nor his senior partner, had succeeded in getting inside Melusine's mind. She had been convinced that they were in the conspiracy to have her certified as 'of unsound mind.'

I had tried to assure her that doctors were singularly loath to certify patients. To do so was, in effect, an admission of failure on their part. In Melusine's case, they were both of the opinion that her miscarriage and hysterectomy were responsible for her withdrawal. 'Traumatic shock' could be used to explain all manner of ills.

Only, as I had begun to see it, Melusine's problem went further back than that. She hadn't had a happy childhood. Her parents had been divorced when she was seven years old. Subsequently, her father had remarried and she had grown up with a fretful, martyred mother.

I fancied that, in both her marriages, Melusine had unconsciously been looking for a father figure. Her first husband had been a widower, twenty years her senior.

The sports car's engine was roaring into life at last. I stubbed out my cigarette — and almost immediately lit another. Why was I feeling this sense of frustration because the man, Gilburn, had finally departed? Had I hoped that he would look in on me again? Now that I had had time to rally from the shock of his revelations, there were a number of questions I would have liked to put to him. I was still in the air about Melusine's new Will and the legacy she had so unpredictably left me. Had it been for any appreciable sum? Not that it mattered. I couldn't accept it, even if I was given the chance — which seemed unlikely. If it amounted to any serious money, her husband would undoubtedly contest the Will, and I imagined that a court would decide in his favour — if it came to a court case. It wouldn't, if I could avoid it. I should be placed in a most invidious position, accused of 'exerting undue influence' on a patient.

I didn't want or need anything from Melusine. With Aunt Elspeth's money and my salary, I was in what Mrs Nocton would call 'comfortable circumstances.' Besides, I knew, as the Colchards would inevitably conclude, that Melusine must have made that Will not from affection for me but from fear of them. It had been a gesture of self-defence. The tragedy of it was that it hadn't protected her.

A tap sounded on my door — and in came Mrs Nocton, carrying a tea-tray. She was flushed and her always wispy grey hair looked as if she had been running her fingers distractedly through it.

"That man!" she ejaculated. "The questions he asked! Not my idea of a policeman. More like what the thrillers call 'a private eye.' Polite enough, but what a nerve!"

"He certainly doesn't lack nerve . . . "

"I thought, if he'd put you through it, too, you'd be glad of a cup of tea."

She set the tray down on my table. I noted that there were two cups and a dish of brandy-snaps. Mrs Nocton knew I had a weakness for brandy snaps . . .

"Two heads are better than one," she added — as if apologizing for the extra cup. She never came into my rooms for tea and a chat unless I invited her. "It seems that there's some mystery about that poor little thing's death and Inspector Gilburn's bent on solving it — but men never see what's right under their noses."

"The police don't think it was an accident," I said, wondering how much Gilburn had told her.

"And it certainly wasn't suicide — so that means foul play," she said breathlessly.

In the intervals of tending her cats and providing me with home comforts, Mrs Nocton was an avid devourer of 'whodunnits.' I sensed that she had been thrilled by Gilburn's interrogation. Her faded blue eyes were sparkling as she poured out tea.

"Why are you sure it wasn't suicide?" I asked.

Sometimes, after we had been for a drive, I had brought Melusine back here for tea but Mrs Nocton had met her only briefly.

"She was going to have one of Amantha's kittens. Remember? She specially asked for a black one, to bring her luck, she said," Mrs Nocton reminded me. "She wouldn't have wanted a kitten or good luck if she'd had it in mind to drown herself. Besides, anyone could see she was a poor frightened little thing. She'd never have taken herself out in a boat, knowing she couldn't swim."

"No. That was definitely out of character," I agreed. "She was inclined to be helpless . . . and she disliked any physical exertion.

I can't picture her launching a boat and rowing or punting it. She would have been more likely to ask someone to take her out on the lake."

"She asked someone she trusted — and so she was off her guard. It wouldn't have taken much strength to drown such a little bit of a thing." She shot a wary glance at me as she handed me a cup of tea. Hitherto, I had shrunk from the topic of Melusine's death and refused to discuss it. "Don't think I'm not sorry for her, Nurse. But . . . since it's happened, all that we can do now is to see that her killer's brought to justice."

"That's a job for the police," I said repressively. "Inspector Gilburn appears to be efficient."

"In his own way, maybe, but whoever read of the police solving this kind of mystery? They just come in at the end, to make the arrest."

"Only this isn't a story," I said, smiling at her eager, animated expression, ridiculously reminiscent of one of her cats when it scented a mouse.

"That's what I told the Inspector when he asked questions about *you*," she proclaimed triumphantly. "I said: 'This isn't one of those stories in which the least probable character did it. You'll have to use your common-sense — *if* you have any. It stands to reason that nobody would kill that pretty little thing for her money, so that rules out anyone who benefits by her Will. Besides, nurses don't kill. It's against their instincts and training.'"

"Oh!" I said, shaken. "He gave you the impression that he suspected *me*?"

"He doesn't know whom to suspect. He's just beating the bushes. I told him he could leave you out of the picture — and Leigh Colchard, too. If you're the least likely, the husband's the most likely — and it never works out that way, either. Besides, it's clear that he knew she'd made a new Will, and that was why they had that quarrel."

"Did the Inspector say that they'd quarrelled?"

"He didn't have to tell me. Why else would her husband have gone off and left the poor little soul alone? You can depend upon it, that's how Leigh Colchard would react," she said with conviction. "He has a fierce temper but he would never lay hands on a woman. He would walk away and then do something strenuous to relieve his feelings."

"You know him?"

"Not to speak to, but I haven't lived in Ashley Combe for twenty odd years without hearing plenty about the Colchards. And I've been over the Nurseries several times. I went last year, with the Ashley Combe Garden Club, and Miss Martina gave us an interesting talk on rose-growing. Then, he showed us round the Nursery. He's a big, fine-looking man. Red-haired and hot-tempered. No patience with fools, but he treats his workers well as long as they play fair by him."

With a pang, I remembered Melusine's weeping in my arms and stammering out that she was 'such a fool.' Had Leigh lost patience with her? But ... to take Melusine out in a boat and drown her hadn't been a spur of the moment, hot-tempered action.

"Have a brandy-snap, dear. You're very pale. Did you let that Inspector upset you?" Mrs Nocton said chidingly. "You mustn't take it personally. See it as a story and try to get at the plot. That's what I mean to do. I've always thought

I could make deductions better than any policeman's."

"He certainly gave me some shocks," I admitted, nibbling a brandy-snap to please her. "Did he tell you that Melusine had made a new Will?"

"He didn't. She told me that, herself. That evening after you'd been to Plymouth. You were changing into your uniform and she was in my sitting-room, playing with Amantha's kittens. I asked her if she'd had a nice day and she said, with a little girl air of mischief: 'I've been making my Will — but it's a secret. You mustn't tell Nurse, because she'd be cross with me, but I've been leaving her a lot of my money. And I've left some to you, so that you can have a high wire fence put up all round the garden and the pussies won't get out into the woods,'" Mrs Nocton quoted. "I said that was very sweet of her — and so it was — but that I was old enough to be her mother and she shouldn't be worrying about a Will at her age. She must have had a premonition."

"She was afraid of her husband and his sister. It was her way of protecting herself."

"The poor dear! Miss Martina has a sharp tongue and I've heard that she didn't approve of her brother's marriage. I dare say she thought he'd be better off without such a helpless wife . . . " She puckered her forehead. "That would be a new slant — but would anyone swallow it? A sister getting rid of her brother's wife isn't really plausible."

"I can't see that killing anyone can ever be plausible. To ordinary people, that is," I said, remembering Gilburn's theory that killers had their own brand of logic.

"It depends how close she is to her brother. With a pretty little thing like that, jealousy has to be the motive."

"Jealousy?" I echoed, startled.

"Much more likely than financial gain," Mrs Nocton said firmly. "That brings us to the stepdaughter. There's always jealousy between a stepmother and a stepdaughter."

"Usually, it's the stepmother who's jealous."

"That's true, but jealousy works both ways. If I were the Inspector, I'd keep a sharp eye on that girl," she pronounced. "More tea, dear? Now, put your feet up for a bit while I see to supper. And not to worry. Leigh Colchard's a fair-minded man, so I've heard. You were very good to his wife, and he won't grudge you a nice legacy. If she'd left money to the doctor instead, that would be another matter. Men can be as jealous as any women."

She trotted out with the tray, leaving the door open. Leo yawned, stretched and jumped down to follow her. Almost immediately, the fluffy semi-Persian, Amantha, stalked in, with two of her kittens prancing after her. One was coal black. That must have been the one Melusine had wanted.

Melusine had been better and less shut up in herself. That she could have remembered Mrs Nocton in her new Will was proof of that. She had sympathized with Mrs Nocton's anxiety about the cats' roaming in the woods. She had liked cats, though she had been nervous of dogs.

The telephone bell was pealing in the small entrance hall. I heard Mrs Nocton answering the call. Then, she popped her head round the door again.

"It's for you, dear. Doctor Badgsworth."

My ankle had stiffened again. I limped out painfully to the telephone. Mrs Nocton, with commendable tact, retreated into the kitchen and closed the door after her.

I lifted the receiver and called: "Hello!"

"Verena? Has that fellow gone?"

"Gilburn? Yes."

"Did he put you through it? Was it very grim?" Tobin asked urgently.

"He gave me a shock or two. Did he tell you that Melusine had left me some money?"

"No. No, I didn't know that. Hell!" he said. "That was all Gilburn needed. He'll be certain now that you were encouraging that wretched woman in her delusions — turning her against her family for your own advantage."

"I tried to talk her out of her fears. If I'd taken them seriously, she might be alive today. Because someone at Weirwater killed her."

"We can't be sure of that. She could have had a sudden fit of acute depression and drowned herself."

"She didn't. She was going to adopt a black kitten of Mrs Nocton's, 'to bring her good luck,'" I said evenly. "Don't fool yourself, Badger. She was murdered. But . . . not by *me*."

"You don't have to tell me that. I'm sorry if I said the wrong thing this evening. I wanted you to know that it wouldn't have made any difference to the way I feel. There has never been anyone else . . . "

"Thank you!"

"For heaven's sake, be careful! When the news of your legacy gets out, you'll have the Colchards gunning for you, too."

He sounded so much concerned that his tone sent a revitalizing current of warmth through me.

"I'll be careful but, like Gilburn, I shan't be satisfied till I get at the truth," I answered. "You'd better watch your step, too. I wouldn't want you to stick your neck out on my account. There's bound to be a lot of talk."

"As if I cared! All I care about is you."

That sounded like the young, impetuous Tobin. I smiled — and then sighed. It had taken him long enough to decide that he still loved me. It was too late now . . . four years too late.

5

IT seemed ironical to reflect that, only twenty-four hours ago, I had pleaded with Matron to let me skip Martina Colchard's lecture. I was eager to meet Melusine's sister-in-law and form my own impression of her.

Not only those who were interested in gardening and flower arrangement but quite a number of our other patients, too, had elected to attend the lecture. As the majority of them were disabled, Matron had decided that Sister Fulbech should accompany the party. The lecture was to be given in St Cuthbert's Parish Hall, in aid of the funds of the Ashley Combe Garden Club.

I had been sent off duty early, to give me time to change. In her determination to banish any suggestion of 'hospitalization,' Hilda Hatherby preferred her staff not to wear uniform when shepherding the patients to any outside function. It wasn't a dictum which endeared itself to Sister

Fulbech. She was one of those tall, gaunt, plain women who looked their best in uniform.

I liked good clothes but Aunt Elspeth had sternly discouraged any 'fussing' over my appearance. Perhaps there had been some truth in Tobin's assertion that she had wanted to 'possess' me. Perhaps she had secretly dreaded that I might marry and leave her. Certainly, she had lost no opportunity of disparaging my looks, insisting that I was too tall for a woman, and too sturdily built, and lamenting my 'cat's eyes' and 'ginger hair.'

My eyes were indubitably an odd shade, somewhere between green and amber, but my hair, ginger in my childhood, had darkened gradually and was now more like ginger-bread than ginger. Certainly, I was tall — five foot nine in my stockings — but my figure had fined down considerably since my 'teens, and I had nicely shaped legs, hands, and feet.

Aunt Elspeth would have called my amber two piece 'hopelessly impractical' but the colour suited me, and both the dress and the coat were elegantly tailored, with that deceptive simplicity of line which costs so much more than frills and fussiness. I had chosen dark amethyst suede shoes, gloves, and handbag to go with the pale amber. On an impulse, I pinned an old amethyst brooch of my grandmother's to the dress and slid a matching amethyst ring on to the third finger of my right hand.

In this, my first encounter with Martina Colchard, I was determined not to look as if I needed any legacies from my patients. Let her see me for what I was — a woman who could earn a good living from her own qualifications and possessed, in addition, a small private income.

At these Garden Club Meetings, tea, coffee and biscuits were served after the lecture. Usually, unless he or she had a train or bus to catch, the speaker mingled with the audience. Our contingent from The Haven frequently came in for special attention, by reason of their wheelchairs and crutches. People, in the main, went out of their way to be kind to the partially disabled — though not always in the right way. I had learnt that most handicapped people were proud of the independence they had so painstakingly achieved, and were disposed to resent clumsy 'helping hands.'

I gave Mrs Nocton a lift as far as the town and then left her to make her own way up Fore Street to the Parish Hall. I drove on to The Haven and parked the Swallowtail. There were several large, especially equipped estate cars belonging to The Haven, in which wheelchairs could be easily transported. I was to drive one of them tonight and Sister Fulbech was to drive another. With one of the porters and a Staff Nurse to help, we set about loading up our party.

"You're looking very smart tonight, Nurse," Staff-Nurse Wilton observed acidly, as she helped me to ease a wheel-chair up the ramp. "Will Doctor Badgsworth be at the lecture?"

I didn't care for Staff-Nurse Wilton. She was only in her early thirties, but she had the embittered outlook of the traditional, frustrated spinster. Sister Fulbech had once told me that 'Harriet Wilton was doing well in a big London hospital. Then she had to make a proper fool of herself over the S.R. — a married man at that. There was quite a furore and she had to leave. She's had a chip on her shoulder ever since'.

"I shouldn't think so," I answered casually. "Doctor Badgsworth isn't a gardening enthusiast."

"You know him well, don't you, Nurse?" she murmured significantly.

"We were at the same training hospital," I reminded her. "Where's Miss Barber? Isn't she coming?"

"No. She has one of her migraines. You've got that ghastly Mrs Thompkin instead. She suddenly decided that she'd like to go. Not that she cares anything about aquatic plants, but she's curious to see Martina Colchard. Really, some women!" Harriet Wilton said in a malice tinged whisper. "Martina Colchard must be as hard as nails. Could you give a talk on water-lilies, when your own sister-in-law had just drowned, picking them? I wonder *you* can face the lecture. She was picking them for you."

"Matron said I must, or I might develop a phobia about water-lilies," I said calmly. "Where is Mrs Thompkin? It's time I started."

"That type always keep people waiting. It makes her feel important," Harriet

Wilton said sourly. "She had the nerve to complain to Matron about me, because she had asked me what I thought of her new hair-style — and I told her. Kiss curls and a camomile rinse at her age!"

"The eternal small, spoilt child," I said. "I must get started. It'll embarrass the wheel-chair contingent if we're late."

"You'll have to wait for Thompkin. She flatly refused to go with Sister. Said you were the only nurse who really understood her," Harriet said nastily. "How do you do it, Frodesley? Induce wealthy patients to feed out of your hand, I mean?"

Was she just trying to sting me . . . or had she heard a rumour about my legacy? I wondered uncomfortably.

"Is Mrs Thompkin wealthy? I imagined that she was dependent on her son," I said evenly.

"The shoe's on the other foot. She owns most of the shares in his father's business."

Sister Fulbech, with the grim expression she always wore when at the driving wheel, was moving off at her usual sedate twenty miles an hour. She was one of those self-termed 'safe' drivers, who crawled along in the middle of the road, ignoring the queue that built up behind her.

"I hope I haven't kept you waiting, Nurse?" Mrs Thompkin came tripping out, resplendent in mink and pearls.

"Nurse Frodesley was about to take off without you," Harriet said. "You'll be suffocated in that fur coat."

"Parish halls are draughty," Mrs Thompkin said, settling herself in the front seat and stroking her mink. "This was my dear husband's last Christmas present to me."

"Broke him?" Harriet said under her breath. "Poor devil!"

"I cannot like that woman," Mrs Thompkin said, as I climbed into the driving seat. "Such an embittered, envious nature."

"Nurse Wilton is very good at radio-therapy," chirped Mrs Baines, the wizened little woman who was squeezed between us. "She has done wonders for my arthritis. Could you move over a shade? You're digging your elbow into my ribs."

"Can't think why you wanted to come, Mrs Thompkin. You're no gardener," observed Miss Haller, a blunt-featured, downright woman, from the back seat. "I wouldn't mind betting that any flowers in your home came from a florist's."

"When my dear husband was alive, we had a very nice garden," Mrs Thompkin retorted. "My husband grew the most heavenly roses. He liked to pretend that Colchard's 'Janetta' was named after me."

"It wasn't. It was after Janetta Colchard," Miss Haller informed her. "Old William Colchard's wife. William was a genius with roses. His son didn't inherit his flair, but Leigh Colchard is a chip off the old block."

"That poor girl's husband? I don't suppose he'll be there tonight," Mrs Thompkin said regretfully.

"Someone will have to show the slides," Miss Haller retorted. "So — that's why you're with us, Mrs Thompkin? Idle curiosity!"

Mrs Thompkin made an aggrieved protest and little Mrs Baines, a born peace-maker, said hurriedly: "Such a tragedy, but Miss Colchard wouldn't have wanted to let the Garden Club down at the last minute."

"They must realize that they're well rid of that little misery," Miss Haller said forthrightly.

I was thankful that it was only a short drive to the Parish Hall. I was shaken by Miss Haller's assumption that Leigh Colchard would be at the Meeting. I had been prepared to encounter his sister. I wasn't ready to face him; the man responsible for Melusine's terror.

The Parish Hall was crowded. It was an open meeting, to which members could bring friends . . . and they appeared to have a great many friends tonight. I felt like echoing Miss Haller's scornful 'idle curiosity.' I was sure that half the people present weren't interested in aquatic plants. They were here to gape at the Colchards; to decide how the Colchards were 'taking it'. Just human nature, of course; the same kind which attracted crowds to the scene of any accident — or crime — but not one of its more endearing manifestations.

Matron had booked seats in advance for our party. The Club secretary had arranged for us to occupy the front row and had left a space at each end for the wheelchairs. I could have wished I was in uniform. A Nurse in uniform was blessedly anonymous and taken for granted. As it was, I felt much too conspicuous as I manœuvred the wheelchairs into position and helped the more mobile of my passengers to seat themselves.

I would have liked to retire to the back of the hall, but that wasn't permissible. I had to be on hand to minister to my contingent if necessary. I found myself awkwardly placed between Mrs Thompkin and Miss Haller, who persisted in talking at each other, across me. They cherished, unhappily, a mutual contempt and aversion. To Miss Haller, an ex-schoolmistress who had lost a leg in a car accident and was struggling to come to terms with her artificial limb, Mrs Thompkin was a tiresome, spoilt baby. Mrs Thompkin complained that Miss Haller was 'bossy, unsympathetic, and positively rude.'

They weren't in the same wing, but nearly all our mobile patients had their meals together in the big dining-room and shared the communal sitting-room and sun lounge, as if The Haven were still an hotel.

The screen for the slides was already in position and the Club secretary, chairman and president were heading for the platform, escorting the guest speaker. When they were seated on the platform, the Chairman rapped sharply on the table — and the murmur of voices died away. He was a retired Colonel and an ardent gardener, a good speaker with a sense of humour. This evening he evidently felt that his mild jokes would be inappropriate. He began by expressing the Club's sympathy with the Colchards in their sad loss, and appreciation of their presence here tonight.

I was barely listening. I was studying Martina Colchard. From Melusine's references to her, I had expected another Miss Haller, but with more malice and aggression. The woman on the platform didn't look either malicious or aggressive. She had a high-boned, horse-shaped face, short-cut, greying auburn hair, and one of those raw-boned, rangy figures which make a woman appear heavier than she really is. She was wearing an undistinguished black dress. Not as a sign of mourning, I guessed, but because it was her standby for occasions like this. From its unfashionable length, the dress was at least two years old. It did singularly little for her figure but I doubted if she had considered that.

To judge from her lack of make-up and boyish haircut, she didn't bother to make the best of herself.

A pity, because her features, if over prominent, were basically good, and she had attractive, almond shaped brown eyes. A good carriage, too, and a clear, pleasant voice, I noted, when she rose to respond to the Colonel's introduction.

She thanked him for his sympathy and said briefly that her sister-in-law's death had certainly been a shock. She had debated with herself whether to come here tonight or not. Some people would probably think her unfeeling . . . but she had decided that it would be more unfeeling of her to let down the hard working officials of the Garden Club.

Also, the days when relatives, after a sudden bereavement, withdrew from the world and observed a strict period of mourning, were long since past . . . and a good thing, too, she added crisply. Idleness never cured or alleviated any blow — and gardeners certainly couldn't afford to be idle while the weeds grew under their feet. She hoped that her talk might induce some of the Club's members to start water gardens; a simple undertaking now that it was possible to construct pools with polythene sheeting. Even a small pool could add interest to a garden and form a pleasing focal point.

As she proceeded to explain the mechanics of constructing an artificial pool, I found myself wondering why Melusine had thought her so formidable. Her clear, concise delivery and her calmly impassive features didn't suggest the violent emotions Melusine had attributed to her.

"Now, if we can have the lights dimmed, we're going to show you some slides," she announced — and a faint ripple appeared to run through the hall as she added: "First, my own water gardens at Weirwater."

Heads turned — and my own turned with them, involuntarily. I had just a glimpse of the projector and slides on a table halfway down the hall, and of a big, red-haired man bending over them. Then, most of the lights were switched off and the first slide appeared on the screen.

I could never, however long I might live, forget that first sight of Weirwater. That incredibly beautiful sheet of water, heavily fringed by trees on two sides, its smooth surface studded with water-lilies, might have been an illustration to a fairy-story. The Frog Prince, I thought instantly. I wished I had nerved myself to take a look at Leigh Colchard before the lights had been switched off, but I hadn't wanted to number myself among those who had been gaping at the newly bereaved husband.

Such a beautiful, peaceful scene . . . but the delicately coloured water-lilies sent a shudder through me. It was among those lilies that Melusine had died. Gasping for breath? Floundering helplessly? Crying out for help . . . with no one to hear? Or forced down and held beneath that smooth water? Who could possibly have committed murder in such a setting?

Martina Colchard was describing various species of water-lilies, with slides, showing them photographed close to, in all their serene, almost waxen beauty. I was beginning to feel sick. There was a horrid, bitter taste in my mouth.

Then, mercifully, Martina went on to irises. More slides of the lake . . . and the weir which had given it its name. There were, indeed, two weirs, the lower one controlled by a sluice gate. The lake, fed by a moorland stream, had been constructed by her great-grandfather, Martina was explaining. Irises had been his main interest and he had been responsible for several hybrids . . .

In other circumstances, I should have been fascinated by the colourful slides of various irises, but now I could concentrate only on the photographs of the lake itself.

There was one glimpse of the house, among the slides, a big grey-stoned house, on a plateau above the lake, with a sloping stretch of grass running down to the water's edge and a blaze of wild yellow irises. Probably there would be pictures of the house and the lake in the sensational newspapers before long; featuring the 'scene of the crime'. If there had been a crime . . .

It seemed incredible, now that I had seen the setting, and was listening to Martina Colchard's efficiently delivered lecture. She was plainly fond and proud of her water garden. Could she, if she knew Melusine's death to be anything except a tragic accident, have talked to us so calmly? Could her brother have brought himself to show those slides?

Yet, according to Inspector Gilburn, it was 'the husband who wasn't satisfied' . . . Not 'satisfied' that it had been an accident, or not 'satisfied' that it had been suicide?

I blinked as the lights flashed on again and Martina asked if there were any questions.

I had a fantastic desire to call out: "Just one. Did you take Melusine out on the lake and drown her?"

There were questions about the price and gauge of polythene sheeting . . . about the cost of water-lilies and how to plant them. People were beginning to shift in their chairs . . . to fidget and exchange comments. I was suddenly conscious that someone was staring hard at me. It was an odd sensation . . . as if X-ray eyes were penetrating my spine. I turned my head — and saw the man, Gilburn, seated three rows behind me. Our eyes met, and he gave me a little bow of acknowledgement.

What was he doing here? I wondered uneasily. Checking up on me — or the Colchards? . . .

Miss Haller was asking an intelligent question about maintenance costs. She was a courageous woman. She fully intended to return to the lonely cottage and garden which she had bought for her retirement, on the verge of Dartmoor.

Martina Colchard had begun to answer the query when Mrs Thompkin suddenly clutched my arm, and gasped that she felt faint.

"Put your head down," I said quickly.

"Don't pay any attention to her, Nurse. She's just playing for it," Miss Haller said bluntly.

"So unkind . . ." Mrs Thompkin quavered — and slid limply down in her chair.

I managed to grab her before she landed on the floor. I tried to support her with one arm and force her head down with my other hand, but, for a small woman, she was both heavy and bulky. I glanced round for Sister Fulbech, but she was at the far end of the row.

"Having trouble? Can I help?"

It was Gilburn who had come to my assistance. He relieved me of the sagging weight on my arm calling: "A glass of water, please. This lady's feeling faint."

Mrs Thompkin's lashes were fluttering. She was too flushed to be in a genuine faint. It must have been the heat which had made her turn dizzy.

There were movements behind us, and a man's voice said: "There's a jug of water on the platform. Hand the jug down, Marty!"

The big red-haired man strode forward to the foot of the platform and Martina leaned down to thrust the water jug into his outstretched hands. He swung round with it. Before I could take it from him, he was dashing cold water on to Mrs Thompkin's hot face.

"Don't! *Don't!*" she spluttered. "You're making me wet."

"Pull yourself together, then, my good woman," he said curtly. "Sit up and drink some water."

Between us Gilburn and I heaved Mrs Thompkin up on the chair, and Leigh Colchard held the jug to her lips. She took a token sip or two — and glowered at him.

"You've poured water down my neck," she complained.

"It appears to have done the trick," he said unsympathetically. "Better get that heavy coat off you . . . "

He was towering over us. He was a

giant of a man with massive shoulders, but a surprisingly slender waist. He had evidently anticipated the heat of the packed hall. He was jacketless, in a crisp white nylon shirt and close fitting black slacks. Mrs Thompkin gaped up at him – and didn't voice any protest as Gilburn and I eased her out of the mink coat.

"Sit tight and I'll bring you some tea," Leigh Colchard said – and strode away.

The Colonel, valiantly endeavouring to ignore the disturbance, had risen, and was thanking Martina for her 'enthralling and instructive talk.'

There was the customary burst of hand-claps – and a brief acknowledgement from Martina. Then the secretary announced that tea, coffee and biscuits were now available.

Mrs Thompkin was dabbing at her damp face with a lace-edged, heavily scented handkerchief.

"I hope I shan't catch a chill," she said plaintively, opening her handbag and getting out her powder compact. "Who was that very rude man? He drenched me."

As if on cue, the 'very rude man' came

striding back to us, bearing a tray loaded with cups of tea and coffee and a dish of sweet biscuits. 'A brute,' Melusine had called him. Certainly, he hadn't an endearing manner, but his forthright tactics had worked.

Mrs Thompkin, having powdered her nose, turned to Gilburn with an apologetic, 'little girl' smile.

"Sorry to have been a nuisance. So kind of you to help," she said graciously. "You're a friend of Nurse Frodesley's?"

"This is Inspector Gilburn, Mrs. Thompkin," I said — and smiled at her start of dismay.

"A policeman?" she gasped — and Miss Haller laughed.

"C.I.D. — but off duty," Gilburn said straightening his slim, impeccably clad figure.

Again, our eyes met, and there was a disarming twinkle in his. It would be easy — fatally easy — to like and trust this man, but Tobin had warned me that Gilburn hadn't accepted my story. He might still be gunning for me.

"Coffee? Tea?" Leigh Colchard was thrusting the tray at us. "Help yourselves."

Mrs Thompkin gave him a baleful stare, but she helped herself to a cup of coffee and three chocolate biscuits.

"Greedy!" Miss Haller said, taking a cup of tea. "We're only supposed to have two biscuits apiece."

"Help yourself!" Leigh Colchard repeated impatiently, as I made no movement towards the tray.

"Patients first," I said primly.

The tray jerked in his hands and, for the first time, he looked directly at me.

"Are you the nurse-in-charge? Sorry! I thought you were one of the patients," he said abruptly.

"Allow me to introduce you," Gilburn said blandly. "Mr Leigh Colchard — Miss Verena Frodesley."

I said formally: "How d'you do?" and braced myself to return his scrutiny.

He had the same high-boned, prominent features as his sister, but there was nothing horse-like about his face. He had a broad forehead and a square, aggressive looking jaw. His hair, a little too long for my taste, was a fiery auburn, but, surprisingly, he had thick brown brows and eyelashes and very dark brown eyes.

"*Frodesley*?" he echoed. "Then . . . you're the girl . . . "

He checked himself, as if belatedly aware of Mrs Thompkin's wide-eyed stare.

"I have to talk to you . . . but not here. I'll give you a ring," he added rapidly, and marched on down the line with his tray.

6

"A VERY rude man. So abrupt, walking off like that," Mrs Thompkin said petulantly.

"Coffee, Miss Frodesley?" Gilburn said invitingly.

With commendable presence of mind, he had whipped two cups of coffee from the tray before Leigh's departure.

"Thank you," I said automatically.

"How do you like the opposition?" Gilburn breathed in my ear. "See what you're up against? You'll have to tread warily."

"Evidently," I said significantly. "Did you say that you were off duty?"

"As far as one ever is. Once a nurse, always a nurse. Once a policeman, always a policeman," he retorted.

The Colonel was escorting Martina from the platform. As they approached the aisle, she stopped short.

"Good evening, Inspector," she said, her lips twisting. "I didn't expect to see you here."

"I enjoyed your talk and the slides were most informative," Gilburn said evenly. "May I introduce Miss Frodesley?"

"*Who*? That nurse?" Martina seemed to shy, like a startled horse. "I've no desire to make her acquaintance."

"Well!" Miss Haller said expressively, as Martina stalked on, after the Colonel. "Talk about manners!"

"And after all Nurse did for that poor girl, too," Mrs Thompkin said indignantly.

Gilburn was smiling . . . 'nastily', Tobin would have said.

"Informative," he murmured.

"Oh, chase yourself!" I flashed, in sudden, uncontrollable exasperation.

Then, as he raised his brows, I felt my cheeks flaming.

"Thank you for your help, but I can manage now," I amended.

"As you wish," he said calmly, and walked away, in his elegant, cat-like fashion.

I bit my lower lip hard. I hadn't intended to snub him, but that smile of his had got under my skin.

"Nurse — " Sister Fulbech advanced upon me, reproof written across her gaunt features. "Mrs Baines and Miss Mitchell haven't had any tea. Couldn't you find some for them? Instead of gossiping with your friend . . . "

"I'm sorry, Sister, but that man . . . " I swallowed down my resentment at her tone. "He isn't a friend of mine. He's a Detective-Inspector . . . "

"So — what? He's also a man, isn't he?" Miss Haller said, as if suspecting me of Mrs Thompkin's brand of snobbery. "An educated and well-bred man at that."

I turned away, clutching my empty coffee cup, my cheeks burning. Surely, Gilburn himself hadn't put that interpretation on my reaction?

I managed to waylay one of the members who was acting as a stewardess. I put my cup on her tray and retrieved two cups of tea.

"The biscuits have all gone. We weren't expecting such a crowd," she said apologetically. "Oh, here's Mr Colchard, with some left!"

Leigh Colchard, carrying a tray of used cups, and the remains of the dish of biscuits, halted at her gesture. He stood there, towering over me, while I hurriedly added biscuits to the saucers. He was the first man I had ever met who seemed to dwarf me. He and Melusine must have looked a ridiculously ill-matched couple on their wedding day.

As the stewardess bustled away, he said jerkily: "When and where can I see you . . . alone?"

"Alone? That sounds ominous," I said with forced lightness.

"We have to talk," he said grimly.

"Well, then, I suppose you could come to my rooms . . . to Mrs Nocton's. Woodlands Cottage. Do you know it?"

"I'll find it," he said. "When? Tonight?"

"Oh, no! I have to take the patients back to The Haven."

"Then, when?"

"I shall be off duty tomorrow evening," I said reluctantly. "I should be home by six. But — "

"Good! I'll be there."

"Why — " I was beginning but, with a curt nod, he was marching on again.

I went back to my patients, with the tea. Mrs Baines thanked me in her usual, deprecating fashion. Miss Mitchell complained that she couldn't eat ginger biscuits.

There were times when patients demanded an exorbitant amount of patience from their long suffering nurses . . . and my stock of patience was running low tonight. Thank goodness, I wasn't on duty tomorrow morning! I could have a good rest.

Only, it didn't work out that way. Tired though I was, I couldn't sleep. I tossed and turned, my head and my ankle aching, those slides of Weirwater seeming to dance in front of my eyes. When I did doze off, I dreamed of the lake and the water-lilies . . . of Melusine and her giant of a husband. Weird, nightmarish dreams. I dreamed that Leigh was grabbing Melusine and tossing her right out into the lake. I plunged in after her but couldn't reach her. The water-lilies were all about me, their slimy leaves and stems clinging to my limbs, so that I couldn't swim.

I woke finally to find Leo lying across my legs and Mrs Nocton trotting in with a tray of tea.

"Looks as if you've had a restless night, dear," she said, pulling up the bedclothes which I had flung half on to the floor. "Take it easy now, and I'll bring you a nice, hot breakfast."

I thanked her but insisted that I would rather get up for breakfast. I felt hot and sticky, in need of a bath and fresh air.

It was as well that I didn't linger in bed. I was smoking an after breakfast cigarette when Mrs Nocton came in with an air of excited expectancy.

"There's a young man to see you, Nurse. Here's his card," she announced. "He says he's from a law firm — Hemp, Milfoil & Agrimony — but he doesn't look like any lawyer I've ever seen. More like one of those Pop singers."

"Oh!" I said, startled. "Well, bring him in, please."

The card looked official enough . . . Hemp, Milfoil & Agrimony. I felt my pulses tingling. The address was that of a street quite close to the Salon where I had taken Melusine. Had she, then, slipped out and called at the first solicitors' whose brass plate she had spotted?

My only previous contact with solicitors had been with Aunt Elspeth's — and he had been a contemporary of her father's. Reputable solicitors should look like grandfatherly figures, or calmly authoritative, like bank managers. I stared incredulously at the young man whom Mrs Nocton ushered into my sitting-room. He looked much too juvenile to be a qualified solicitor and anything but 'legal.' He was wearing a conventional dark suit, but with a be-ruffled pale blue shirt under it. His glossy fair hair was worn low over his forehead and down to the nape of his neck.

"Miss Frodesley?" he inquired, advancing upon me with outstretched hand and a flashing smile which displayed fine, even white teeth. "I'm Maurice Agrimony. I hope you don't mind my popping in on you like this, but the position's a bit sticky and my uncle — that's George Agrimony, one of the senior partners — thought it might be an idea for me to contact you unofficially first."

Another 'unofficial' visit?

"How d'you do?" I said. "Do sit down."

He gave my hand a warm shake and then sank gracefully on to the sofa.

"Thanks! I'm definitely in the dog-house over this Colchard affair. With my seniors, that is," he said, with an engaging air of candour. "They're all tied up in green tape and never, but *never* perform the simplest action 'without due consideration' as they call it. You can't convince them that this is the jet and space age."

"That must be a trial to you, Mr Agrimony."

He looked about twenty-one, but I supposed he must be at least twenty-five. He had an almost girlishly fair clear skin, and wide, attractively blue eyes.

"You can bet your life it is!" he said feelingly. "I can't stand all that dilly-dallying and solemn conferences over every trifle. Why shouldn't our business be run as swiftly and efficiently as any other? Why cloak it in mystery and hide-bound phrases? I'm doing my best to clear away the cobwebs, but it's tough going."

"I see. About Mrs Colchard — " I prompted him.

"I was just leading up to her. I was the only one of us in the office when she called and insisted that she had to make her Will then and there. She was all het up and very much beauty in distress. Not having a heart locked away in a safe deposit, I had to humour her," he explained. "According to my seniors, my behaviour was unprecedented and madly unconventional. They never, but *never*, draw up Wills without preliminary drafts and endless nattering."

"No?"

"Definitely no. But . . . there was this lovely girl, agitated but grimly determined. If I'd put her off, she would have marched out and gone to another firm. She just wouldn't wait. She said she dared not; that her husband was planning to kill her and that she wouldn't be safe till she'd made a new Will. Well, what would you have done, Miss Frodesley? Shown her to the door?"

I shook my head. Melusine, frightened and pleading, had been irresistible.

"I thought she'd just had the hell of a row with the said husband and was out to get her own back," Maurice Agrimony said frankly. "My guess was that she wanted this new Will to brandish at him and bring him to heel. Then, they would fall into each other's arms, and the Will would end up in the wastepaper basket. I didn't fall for that talk of his meaning to murder her. Murder's so messy — and damn' risky, too."

"Yes. Certainly."

"But, it can happen — and it looks as if, this time, it did. That Inspector chap is pretty close-mouthed, but I could guess what he was thinking. My seniors are simply livid. The firm has never been involved in a murder case in all its respectable, reputable century of operations. 'Too late to worry about that now, and who shrinks from a spot of publicity these days?' I've been assuring them," he grinned. "Anyway, the Will's perfectly legal and straightforward. I've brought a copy for you."

"Just tell me what's in it," I said hurriedly, as he produced a document from his inside jacket pocket and held it out as if offering a biscuit to a dog.

"It's utterly simple. One thousand pounds to Mrs Nocton of this address 'for the erection of a high wire fence'. Everything else to Miss Verena Frodesley 'who has shown me the only disinterested kindness and affection which I have ever received.' She insisted on that phrase."

"Everything?" I caught my breath. "The Inspector talked of a handsome legacy. Not of 'everything'."

"You're what's called the residuary legatee, which means that you scoop the pool," he assured me. "Very nice, too, even after death duties. Of course, I didn't know Mrs Colchard from the original Eve. She might only have had a few Savings Certificates to leave. I took the whole affair as a typically feminine gesture."

"Yes," I said slowly. "I can understand that."

"It was just my luck — or yours — that my uncle wasn't around when she called. He would have recognized her as the former Mrs Henry Elland. You've heard of Elland's Fertilizers? Taken over by one of the big general combines after Henry Elland's death."

I shook my head dazedly.

"Then . . . there is a lot of money, Mr Agrimony?"

"At a guess, around £250,000, less the death duties."

"Hell!" I said helplessly. "I can't possibly take Melusine Colchard's money. We weren't even distantly connected."

"If he killed her, the husband can't take it, either. If he didn't, he's bound to contest the Will," Maurice Agrimony said cheerfully. "Not to worry. You're in the clear . . . unless, of course, you drowned her?"

"I certainly didn't. I hadn't the vestige of a motive, anyway. She didn't tell me about the Will."

"No? She meant to tell her family. She left the original with me, but she took a copy of it with her."

"I suppose the Inspector found it among her papers," I said. "He and another policeman went through her things. Looking for a suicide note, they said."

"She didn't commit suicide. She was looking forward to tantalizing her family with that Will. She'd quite cheered up when she left the office," he observed shrewdly. "Too bad that it didn't come off as she had planned. I'm glad I'm not in her husband's shoes. Has he an alibi?"

"A vague kind, I believe."

"If it looked cast-iron, he would be patently guilty. I say, it's all rather a thrill, isn't it?" he said with an exuberant grin. "Should shake the old fogeys up a bit. My uncles, that is; George Agrimony and Maurice Milfoil. Do you want us to act for you? Or have you a tame solicitor of your own?"

"No. Only my late aunt's — and he's two hundred miles away. He wouldn't care to be brought into this, anyway," I said wryly. "He's over seventy and very precise."

"Oh, good! Then, you can hire *me* to safeguard your interests," he said persuasively. "I'll be right on the ball. I won't let the Colchards put anything over on you. Or that Inspector chap, either."

"Thank you! If I should need a solicitor, I might take you up on that," I said tentatively.

"You'll need one. They'll all be after you like a pack of hounds. The Press, too," he warned me. "There can't have been a sensation like this in Ashley Combe for years. 'Murdered Wife Leaves Fortune to Sympathetic Nurse.' Can't you see the headlines?"

I felt myself flinching. I had had enough publicity at the time of Aunt Elspeth's death . . . but, at least, the police and the Coroner had been satisfied with my account of the accident.

"There was talk, so Uncle George told me, after Henry Elland's death. Rumours that he'd killed himself from jealousy over his lovely young wife. There were even suggestions that she'd fed him the phenobarbitone because he'd refused to give her a divorce," Maurice announced. "Only, no other man materialized, so, in the end, it was brought in as 'death by misadventure'. Odd if she did murder her first husband and then got herself murdered."

"*Don't*! She could never have murdered anyone. She was much too helpless and impractical."

"A born victim? I imagine that she could be provoking. So quietly persistent. You know?"

"I didn't really know her all that well . . . "

"This'll give your old dears at The Haven a kick. Me, too," he said, grinning again.

"*Don't*! What on earth will Matron say?"

"She'll probably be green with envy. Incidentally, have you made a Will?"

I nodded, my cheeks beginning to burn. Aunt Elspeth's solicitor had insisted that I must make my Will. I had thought that absurd, at my age, but to humour him, I had agreed. Perhaps as a belated gesture of defiance to my aunt, I had named Tobin Badgsworth as my 'residuary legatee.'

Now . . . my brain was reeling under the implications. If I were to be killed in a car smash today, Tobin would presumably drop in for Melusine's money. Of all the involved, impossible situations! I would have to make another Will in the Colchards' favour, just in case anything happened to me before all this business was sorted out satisfactorily. Unless . . . suppose one of them had killed her?

The Colchards hadn't, in any event, any real claim on Henry Elland's money. It should go to his own daughter. But . . . Melusine must have thought of that. Had she had any specific reason for willing it away from her stepdaughter?

"That's O.K., then! As long as you haven't made your Will in Leigh Colchard's favour. It would be a pity if *you* were found floating in that sinister lake, Miss Frodesley," Maurice said — only half in jest, I fancied. "I'd better push off now. I'm completing a purchase at noon. I get all the dreariest chores. You're a welcome diversion."

There was something cheering about this irrepressible, lighthearted young solicitor. If I had to have a solicitor, I would certainly prefer him to a more traditional type. He wouldn't get me tied up in pompous legal phrases. He was in my own age group.

"You needn't be afraid that I don't know my stuff," he added. "Our exams are pretty stiff, and I've had quite a bit of practical experience."

"One does tend to think of lawyers as having been born middle-aged," I admitted. "But I'm sure you'll — what's the phrase? — 'protect my interests', should the necessity arise."

"Thanks! It will arise, 'as sure as eggs is eggs'. There's too much money at stake for the Colchards to sit back with folded hands and wish you luck," he said darkly. "Let me know if they approach you."

"Leigh Colchard is coming to see me this evening."

"He is? At his request, presumably?"

I nodded — and for the first time, he looked grave.

"That could be dangerous. I ought to be here."

"I'd better see him alone and find out what's in his mind," I said reluctantly. "A solicitor present would put his hackles up and we shouldn't get anywhere."

"Well, don't promise him anything. If he gets fierce, just give me a ring and I'll be right over."

7

"**D**ANGEROUS?" The word seemed to echo and re-echo in my ears, after Maurice Agrimony had roared away, in his colourful little car with its obviously souped up engine, but I didn't anticipate any physical danger. What good could it do Melusine's family to eliminate me?

No. The danger to me and my future was more subtle and insidious than that. I was squirming inwardly at the prospect of the publicity Maurice was gleefully anticipating. If, when the inquest was resumed, a verdict of 'murder by person or persons unknown' was brought in, the heat would be switched on with a vengeance. To date, Melusine's death hadn't attracted more than a brief, non-committal paragraph in the papers. Ostensibly, it had been a simple case of accidental drowning. Whoever had clasped her hand round those water-lilies must be cursing himself or herself now. Without that pointer, would even the perceptive Gilburn have suspected that she hadn't taken the boat out and overturned it?

Or had it been the fact that Melusine had been recovering from a 'nervous breakdown' at The Haven which had aroused Gilburn's suspicions? Was that why he had questioned me so relentlessly on his initial visit to The Haven? Had I said something to deepen his misgivings? I couldn't remember now what I had told him. I had been too badly shocked and shaken by the news to measure my words.

I believed that, however long it took him, and no matter how many lives were disrupted in the process, Gilburn would arrive at the truth. There was a savage satisfaction in that thought, but it couldn't save my hide for me; couldn't protect me from the floodlights.

Hilda Hatherby was proud of the fact that no breath of scandal had ever touched The Haven. Since her only mistake had been in sending Melusine home for the weekend, The Haven was still in the clear, but I wasn't, and I was on the staff. How could Hilda keep The Haven out of the headlines? Melusine would certainly be written up as 'a mental case', and I as the unscrupulous nurse who had taken advantage of her 'disturbed' condition.

Matron would be on the spot. If she dismissed me summarily, it would look as if she believed me to be guilty of exploiting my position. Yet, if she kept me on, the floodlights would be directed on to The Haven. It was only fair to warn her, before the news broke.

Parrying Mrs Nocton's excited questions about Maurice Agrimony's visit, I changed hurriedly into uniform. I must try to see Matron before I went on duty.

I managed to catch her after she had completed her daily tour of inspection. She didn't appear surprised by my request for an interview. Perhaps she had heard rumours . . .

"Sit down, Nurse," she said cordially. "How did you enjoy the lecture last night?"

"It was very interesting."

"And you weren't sick after all?"

There was a quizzical gleam in the grey eyes behind her glasses. I jerked up my chin.

"No. Because I don't feel so wretchedly

guilty now. If Melusine hadn't been drowned, something else would have happened to her," I answered. "One of her own family wanted her out of the way . . . just as she told me."

Matron raised her brows.

"Aren't you allowing your imagination too free a rein?"

"Inspector Gilburn believes that she was deliberately drowned."

"Is that so? Unpleasant for all concerned."

"I don't suppose it was exactly pleasant for Melusine," I retorted. "But . . . I came to ask you, Matron, what you would like me to do . . . "

She heard me out in silence.

When I'd finished, she said crisply: "Thank you for being frank with me, Nurse. It's an awkward position for you, but you'll just have to sit tight, until the police have completed their investigations. If they prove that Leigh Colchard engineered his wife's death, then it'll be clear that she had every justification for willing the money away from him."

"And if he isn't guilty?"

"Possibly you will feel disposed to make some settlement in his favour . . . but you'll have to take legal advice on that point," she said judicially.

"If you would like me to leave . . . "

"Do you wish to leave? On the strength of your legacy?"

"Oh, no! I would hate to give up nursing, and I've been happy here. Whatever happens, I can't accept Melusine's money. I'm sure she made that Will just to protect herself," I said hurriedly. "Would it mean less publicity for you if I went away?"

"I doubt if the police would allow you to leave Ashley Combe," she said dryly. "As the main beneficiary, you must be on their list of suspects. My advice to you, Nurse, is to carry on as usual. If the pressure becomes acute, you might take a fortnight's leave, but there's no question of your being asked to resign. Good nurses aren't ten a penny. You get on well with our patients."

"Thank you! Honestly, I had no idea what Melusine was planning," I said confusedly.

"No," she said. "I'm sure you hadn't. 'Casting bread on the waters,' wasn't it? One can only hope that most of this loaf isn't nibbled away in lawyer's fees."

"I didn't take Melusine's talk of 'a lot

of money' seriously. I supposed her first husband's money would be tied up for his daughter."

"Odd that it wasn't. If you do inherit this fortuitous legacy, you might care to invest some of it here," she said reflectively. "I would like to add a heated swimming bath to our other amenities."

She was certainly a shrewd business woman. Had the estimated size of my legacy coloured her attitude towards me? It might have crossed her mind that, to keep me on and stand by me during the inevitable, forthcoming publicity, might be to her advantage.

"Don't let yourself be bounced or persuaded into relinquishing your legacy," Hilda Hatherby warned me. "And don't worry yourself sick. That Inspector wants to make a major case of Melusine Colchard's death, but it wouldn't surprise me if it did turn out to be an accident."

"She didn't take that boat out on her own."

"Whoever was with her could have failed to save her and then panicked."

I didn't realize it, as I thanked her and departed, but I had the whole solution in my hands then. Men were wont to scoff at feminine intuition, but the women who had known Melusine had guessed how and why she had died. If I had paused to put the pieces together, I could have saved myself a lot of headaches and heartaches.

Sister Fulbech pounced on me with transparent relief.

"You're late, Nurse . . . but I'm certainly glad to see you," she hailed me.

"Sorry, Sister! I was with Matron," I answered. "What can I do for you, specifically?"

"Cope with Mrs Thompkin. She's lying on her bed, crying herself into hysterics. She won't tell me what's upset her. She says I wouldn't understand." Sister gave a snort. "Too right! If you ask me, she needs a good old-fashioned spanking. Try if you can sort her out!"

Accordingly, I made my way up to Mrs Thompkin's pleasant, sunny bedroom. The curtains had been drawn and I could only just distinguish her plump, heaving body prostrate on her bed.

"Mrs Thompkin?" I laid a tentative hand on her shoulder. "Have you had bad news?"

"Terrible! I can't bear it . . . " She gasped, and turned over on to her back. "Oh, Nurse, I'm so thankful you're here!"

"You mustn't cry like this. You'll give yourself a headache. Sit up and let me bathe your face. Then, I'll get you a good strong cup of tea," I said, in the tone I would have used to a weeping child. "You've had a shock? A letter? From your son?"

"Yes. The most terrible letter. Oh, I knew you would understand! You're so sympathetic . . . "

It hadn't needed any great brain-power to arrive at that simple deduction. Nobody, except her only son, mattered to Mrs Thompkin. Since he never visited her during his office hours, it was obvious that he must have written to her.

"He might have told me, when he was here the other evening. So unkind and cowardly to write and give me such a shock. It was that girl's idea, I don't doubt. She'll never let him go now."

She allowed me to raise her into a sitting position, and submitted like a forlorn child to my ministrations.

"Let's have a little sunshine," I said, when I had bathed her swollen eyelids and tear-blotched face. "Everything seems worse in the dark. What did your son tell you? That his wife is going to have a baby?"

She drew a quick, deep breath.

"How clever of you, Nurse!" She reached under the pillows and produced a crumpled, tear-blotted letter. "Read what he says. How could he write to his own mother like that?"

I drew back the curtains and reluctantly applied myself to the letter; the letter of a weak and cowardly man, who had been a shuttlecock between two possessive women for too long.

Sally and he were delighted at the prospect of a baby, he had written. So Vic's wife had a name of her own? 'Sally?' 'Sally' was a friendly sounding pet name — but this Sally evidently had nothing but a resentful animosity towards her mother-in-law. Sally had to take things easily and mustn't be worried or agitated, as her blood pressure was a little high. Vic was sure his mother would realize that there could be no question of her coming home. Sally's welfare had to be his primary consideration now.

"They don't want me. They could hardly make that clearer," Mrs Thompkin said plaintively. "They're trying to thrust me right out of their lives."

"It isn't a very kind letter, but it's the first baby they're expecting," I said. "Women do get odd fancies at such a time and your son obviously feels that he has to humour his wife. It'll be different after the baby's born."

"Different? How?"

"When the first thrill wears off, they'll find the baby a tie. Grandmothers are always in demand as baby-sitters."

"They'd never trust me with their precious baby."

"Why not? You've had a baby and reared him successfully," I reminded her.

"We were badly off when Vic was born. I had to do everything for him," she said, brightening visibly. "I spoilt him, and I'm paying for it now, but he was a healthy, sturdy little boy."

"You'll be having another little boy in the family . . . to carry on your husband's business," I said persuasively. "Now, powder your nose while I get some tea for you."

When I returned with the tea-tray and some chocolate biscuits, she had roused herself to repair the ravages of her emotional stress.

She said, with unfamiliar resolution: "You're quite right, Nurse. I oughtn't to let that hysterical girl's fancies upset me. I'm not going to force myself on anyone who doesn't want me. I shall stay here till after the baby's born. Then . . . we shall see."

"I'm sure that's the sensible thing to do."

"They'll realize later how much I can do for the child, provided I'm given the chance." Her small mouth hardened. "If that wife of Vic's persists in her bitter, jealous attitude towards me, they'll regret it. I shan't leave them any more than I'm obliged to, under the terms of my husband's Will. I shall leave all the rest to you, Nurse."

"Oh, no!" I protested. "You mustn't do that."

"Why not? I'm really attached to you. You understand me. I may live to be an old woman, but one never knows. I might suddenly collapse," she pronounced.

"I should like to feel I had given you something to remember me by . . . and, with money of your own, you could get our attractive doctor away from that Elland girl."

"Please put that idea out of your head! I wouldn't want to buy myself a husband," I said hastily.

"I shall write to my solicitor," she said obstinately. "Vic needs a sharp lesson. He doesn't appreciate all I've done for him. He should have stood up to that wife of his. She made him write that cruel letter."

Her lips were quivering again.

"Have a chocolate biscuit!" I said, as if to a child. "They're your favourite kind, with cream in the centre. And don't let your tea get cold . . . "

"She could have been a daughter to me . . . but did she ever take the trouble to consider my tastes? There's no kindness in her — and one does appreciate kindness as one gets older," she said, biting into a biscuit.

8

I HAD often thought that people's choices of cars, as of pets, was revealing. It betrayed facets of their character which were not apparent in other directions. When I heard a car draw up at Mrs Nocton's gate, I wished I could see it from my sitting-room.

She tapped on my door and announced excitedly: "He's here! He's just coming up the path. Now, be careful, Nurse dear."

"If I need help, I'll scream," I said dryly. "What's his car, Mrs Nocton?"

"It isn't what you'd call a car. It's one of those farm things. You know. A Land Rover."

A Land Rover? Yes. That would be appropriate to such a giant of a man, I thought swiftly; physically, that was. Mentally? Land Rovers were utility vehicles, powerful and reliable, but not spectacular or fast. The adventurous type, who wanted to cut a dash and wasn't too scrupulous in his treatment of other road users, wouldn't choose a Land Rover. Absurd to reason this way, perhaps, but I was convinced that a man who would marry a pretty, fragile widow for her late husband's money, wouldn't be content with a Land Rover.

I had expected Leigh Colchard to drive a Mercedes or an open Bentley or at least a Jaguar. A Land Rover caused me to revise my mental picture of him. It would, of course, be useful for transporting his rose bushes. Did that mean that his rose growing came first with him, and appearances a long way second? Had he no desire for the impeccably tailored suits and the discreetly expensive and speedy car on which Gilburn had expended his godmother's legacy?

"I've always preferred my pussies, but there are times when a big, fierce-looking dog would be handy," Mrs Nocton said feelingly. "We could both be murdered here, and there'd be no one to hear our screams."

A sudden, sharp rapping sounded on the front door.

"Let Mr Colchard in, please . . . and not to worry. He's come to open negotiations, not to threaten," I said hurriedly.

"Well, don't listen to him. That poor little thing knew what she was doing."

That was a moot point. Melusine had been frightened . . . and with good cause, so it would seem . . . but, as that irrepressible young solicitor had pointed out, to drown his wife in his own lake in full view of the house would have been an insane risk for Leigh Colchard to have taken. Was a man who bought himself a Land Rover the type to take insane risks?

He walked into the sitting-room as if he owned it. He had that kind of unconsciously lordly, arrogant bearing.

He took my hand in a brief, firm clasp and said: "Good evening, Miss Frodesley! Thank you for letting me come. You're probably tired after your day's work. I'll try not to keep you long."

I was surprised by that much consideration. I had taken it for granted that he would regard me with implacable hostility — and show it.

"Sit down, won't you? Sherry?" I said, moving to the sideboard.

"Thanks!"

He didn't attempt to dispense the sherry in Gilburn's polished manner. He flung himself into a deep leather-covered arm-chair.

"Mind if I smoke?" he asked, producing a large briar and a battered looking tobacco pouch.

"Of course not. Go ahead!"

I handed him a cut crystal glass of Amontillado. As he thanked me, the thought crossed my mind that he would have preferred a tankard of beer. He was poles apart from Gilburn — or Tobin. He didn't even cast a cursory glance around the room, let alone appraise its furnishings, after Gilburn's fashion. He looked directly at me, as I seated myself on the sofa, facing him.

He evidently wasn't out to impress me. He was wearing a worn sports jacket, rubbed at the elbows, a faded green high-necked sweater, and brown drill slacks. He had brushed back his over-long, fiery red hair but his square chin had a bristly look, as if it was in need of a shave.

"First," he said abruptly, "I have to thank you for your kindness to my wife."

That startled me. It was the last thing I had expected.

"Oh, yes!" he said, as if registering my

surprise. "She talked about you . . . sung your praises. She didn't get on well with her own sex, so I guessed you must be an exceptionally good nurse. I was thankful that she had found a friend at last. She always seemed so much alone, poor kid! It was as if she couldn't come to terms with the world at large."

Again, I was startled. I hadn't expected such perception from him, any more than I had expected this calmly friendly tone. I eyed him warily. Was that his way of disarming me; softening me up before he cracked down on me? Or didn't he know about Melusine's fantastic Will? He must know . . .

He was pausing, as if for my comments. "Had she always this difficulty in communication?" I asked. "I gathered that she was the only child of a broken marriage. She seemed to feel the loss of her father acutely."

"Yes. And she blamed her mother for it. Specifically, her mother's having had a hysterectomy." Furrows showed up deeply across his broad forehead. "It was after her own hysterectomy that things went wrong for us. Melusine fancied that the pattern was repeating itself. She couldn't forgive me for having consented to the operation — but I was assured that it was a 'must'. I couldn't risk her life . . . "

"Naturally not. Were you desperately anxious for a son?"

"Good heavens, no! That was just one of the poor kid's obsessions. Apparently, her father had yearned for a son — and had one by his second wife. Henry Elland, too, was disappointed that Reine was a girl and had hoped that Melusine would give him a son." The furrows deepened and he made an expressive gesture of distaste with his half-filled pipe. "If only Melusine had found the courage to tell me that, after her first miscarriage, she had been warned not to try again, all this trouble might have been avoided."

"Might it?"

"I suppose most men would like a son to carry on after them, but I hadn't any strong feelings on the subject," he said impatiently. "It was she who was so passionately anxious to have a baby . . . or rather a son. It was as if she felt compelled to justify her existence."

"To you . . . or to her father?"

"That's a good question! My theory is that most of her unfortunate tendencies could be traced back to her father's abandoning her when she was at an impressionable age. She felt that she, as well as her mother, must have failed him."

I nodded. He was pressing tobacco into his pipe, tamping it down with firm, blunt finger-tips. His glass of sherry stood untouched on the small rosewood table at his elbow. There was a frowning intensity about his high-boned features and his abstracted concentration on his pipe.

Driven by a curiosity beyond my control, I asked: "Why did you marry Melusine, Mr Colchard?"

He jerked up his head as if I'd flicked him with a whip-lash. For a moment, his very dark eyes seemed to smoulder at me. Then, he shrugged his massive shoulders.

"It was a mistake, of course, but I'm not a clairvoyant. I couldn't foresee that I was the wrong man for her. She seemed so pitifully vulnerable and alone . . . so devastated by Henry Elland's death. She clung to me . . . " he said slowly.

"Oh? You knew her before his death?"

"Didn't she tell you that? He was a friend of my father's. I'd known him for years. He was of my father's generation rather than mine, but he was good to me after my father died. Things were in a bit of a mess. My father wasn't much of a business man," he said jerkily. "Henry Elland insisted on helping . . . giving me an interest free loan till I could get the Nurseries ticking over again. Naturally, I was grateful to him."

"I see."

"Do you? Even after I'd repaid the loan, there was a sense of obligation. He seemed to like me to visit him — he wasn't a man who made friends easily. For a wealthy man, he lived a peculiarly isolated kind of existence. When he died, Melusine and Reine both turned to me, as if they hadn't anyone else . . . "

This was an aspect of Melusine's second marriage which I hadn't glimpsed before. It hadn't dawned on me that Leigh Colchard might have married her from compassion.

"You weren't in love with her?"

Again, he gave that sudden upward jerk of his head — and I felt myself flushing.

"I'm sorry," I said swiftly. "I've no

earthly right to ask such personal questions . . . but I was fond of Melusine."

"So was I, believe it or not." He gave me a twisted grimace of a smile. "She was so small and helpless and appealing. I didn't realize that in many ways she had remained a child — that she craved for a father's love and protection and wasn't constitutionally capable of a man-woman relationship. She clung to me, and I suppose I was flattered as well as touched. It wasn't her fault that I should have known better."

"That's generous of you . . . "

I added inwardly: 'If you mean it . . . '

He sounded sincere, but he might be putting on an act. It didn't seem in keeping with what I had heard of him that he should talk so freely to a stranger or answer such pertinent questions without resentment.

"Generous?" He jerked his head again. "Certainly not. I was anything but generous to that poor kid. I grudged her the time and attention and — er — the emotional responses she demanded. Finally, when I was wearied to death by the whole sticky mess, I sent her to The Haven. Admittedly, it was at Dr Hurst Green's urging — but that doesn't absolve me of my responsibility. She felt that I was rejecting her. Possibly, I was. Who's to say?"

He struck a match and applied it to his pipe, shielding it with his big, squarish hands, as if he were accustomed to lighting a pipe in a strong breeze. He was essentially an out-of-doors character, I surmised. He had that tough, weathered, forceful air, often noticeable in men who did constant battle against the elements. A ridiculously incongruous partner for Melusine, who had been a hothouse plant.

He got the pipe going to his satisfaction and then glanced directly at me again.

"Well? I've answered your questions because I owe you something for doing for Melusine what I failed to do. Now, it's your turn to answer mine."

"Go right ahead!" I said, bracing myself. "Not that I can tell you much. Melusine slipped away from me when we were at the hairdresser's in Plymouth. She didn't warn me then — or subsequently — that she had been to Milfoil, Hemp and Agrimony."

"How much?" he said blankly. "Come again!"

"The Plymouth solicitors. You must have heard that she went to them to make that fantastic Will."

"Oh, that?" Again he made an expressive gesture with his pipe. "No need to go into legal matters at this point."

I blinked at him.

"No need?" I echoed incredulously. "Isn't that why you're here? To discuss her Will?"

"Hell, no! What on earth d'you think I am?" Now, at last, there was the note of savagery in his tone for which I had been sub-consciously waiting. "Until all this mystery about the poor kid's death is cleared up, how can you expect me to concern myself about her Will?"

I felt as if he had slapped me.

"It was such an extraordinary Will," I said defensively. "You know that she left virtually everything to me?"

"I knew that was her intention. She told me so . . . that last afternoon. Well? What was I supposed to do about it? She could do what she pleased with her own money."

"Is that what you told her?" I said unbelievingly.

He scowled at me.

133

"What else? Except that it seemed a bit tough on Reine — since Reine's father had made the money. That set her off, into one of her emotional, incoherent tirades against Reine. She insisted that Reine was responsible for Henry Elland's death, for the loss of both babies, and for turning me against her — and goodness knows what more! It was useless to reason with her. I just got up and walked away . . . may heaven forgive me! I shouldn't have left her, but I'd heard it all before. There was always some woman — her own mother or Reine or my sister — conspiring against her and 'spoiling everything' for her. You were the one exception; the only woman she ever trusted."

He shot the words at me with a leashed bitterness and violence, as if he were pressing the trigger of a machine-gun.

"I didn't know — " I said, but he went on with the same relentless rapidity: "Ironical if you were the one who drowned her, as that Inspector fellow appears to suspect. Not convincing, though. Not from a nurse. You'd have to have been a pretty despicable character to have wormed your way into her affections, induced her to make that Will, and then killed her. Devilishly clever, too. Knowing Melusine, I assured the Inspector that, if you'd even hinted at a legacy, she would instantly have changed her mind about you."

"Thank you," I said weakly, trying to rally from the hail of words. "What — what do you think happened?"

"That's what I came here to discuss. I believe the poor kid was deliberately drowned — and I have to know by whom. You can refuse to answer, but I shall inevitably draw my own conclusions from your silence," he said grimly.

"Now you sound like a policeman," I said, bewildered. "What questions can you have to put to me? I've already been grilled by Gilburn."

"I want to know the truth about this affair of Melusine's with the doctor. How far had it gone?"

"With the doctor?" I gaped at him. "What doctor?"

"Is there more than one romantically handsome, fascinating young doctor around here?" he demanded contemptuously. "It's too late to try to cover up for Dr Badgsworth — though I understand that you're another

135

of his girl friends. Exactly how much was there between him and Melusine?"

"You're crazy!" I said indignantly. "There wasn't anything at all between them."

"Cut out the shocked indignation," he said roughly. "Melusine herself told her step-daughter about it. She was nerving herself to ask me for a divorce, so that she could marry Badgsworth."

"Oh, no!" I said, appalled. "That's sheer, distorted imagination on someone's part. Tobin Badgsworth wasn't remotely interested in your wife, except as a patient."

"You believe that? Yes, obviously, you do. Sorry if I've given you a shock." Again, he gave me a twisted smile. "I should have guessed that neither of them would tell you about their affair. You would be what's called an 'interested party'."

"There was nothing to tell. Do you take me for a fool?" I flashed. "I was looking after Melusine. If she had been in love with Tobin, I should have seen it."

"Not necessarily. She could be inhumanly secretive."

"One senses these things. Anyway, Tobin would have told me. We discussed Melusine's condition repeatedly. You don't understand doctors. That's quite evident," I said, exasperated. "They do sometimes fall for a patient — but not that kind of patient. To Tobin, Melusine's case history was deeply interesting. Not Melusine as a woman. Tobin's the last man who would go for that helpless, super-sensitive, clinging type, even if he hadn't thought her pretty sick, mentally and emotionally."

"You may have something there, but he certainly gave her the impression that he was in love with her. And that's why he's my Number One suspect," Leigh said forthrightly. "She was a born clinger . . . and she had begun to cling to him. He could have panicked, realizing what any scandal could do to him professionally."

"Oh, really, Mr Colchard! That's even more fantastic than the Inspector's suspicions of me," I protested.

"Is it? If, as Gilburn imagines, Badgsworth was planning to marry you, would he let you guess that Melusine was becoming a menace to him?" There was a look in his dark eyes now — a flicker of compassion — which stung me. "Isn't it true that he dissuaded you from visiting us on Sunday afternoon? That he took you up on the

137

moors instead? Then, brought you back here at six o'clock? He could have driven straight to Weirwater after he'd left you, not intending to kill Melusine but to reason with her. She wanted those water-lilies for you and she wouldn't have hesitated to let him row her out on the lake."

"Don't!" I said, shaken by the picture he was etching.

It couldn't be true. Of course, it wasn't true. But . . . given his false premises, it just might have happened that way. I couldn't deny that Tobin had been determined to keep me away from Weirwater, or that he hadn't tried to deter me from getting back in time for church.

"I believe the doctor attempted to convince Melusine that he hadn't any idea of marrying her. She would have reacted dramatically. She might even have thrown herself into the water, to scare him." Leigh Colchard's lips tightened. "He didn't have to touch her. He could just have rowed back to shore — then turned the boat loose."

"Horrible! Monstrous!" I said, flinching. "It's not possible. Tobin could never have left a helpless woman to drown. Besides, someone would have heard her screams

138

... and his car ... "

"There was nobody within earshot of the lake. Reine does remember that she heard a car start up, but she didn't pay any attention to it. People frequently stop and stroll into our woods for a glimpse of the lake and the house — or drive up to the nurseries to look at the roses."

"Reine ... " I echoed. "You're not querying her evidence ... but she could be lying. It was Reine who gave you this monstrous story about Melusine and Tobin?"

"Melusine herself hinted that, if I no longer loved her, there were other men in the world." He drew hard on his pipe, sending out puffs of smoke, as if erecting a smoke-screen behind which to conceal his emotions. "She had this pathetic craving to be constantly reassured that she was loved. I didn't understand that she couldn't help it. I found it rather nauseating. I'm not trying to defend myself ... just explaining why she might have attached herself to that attractive young doctor."

"He wouldn't have given her any encouragement. He's had too much experience. Right back in his student days, Tobin had girls flinging themselves at his feet. He learned how to cope with them. Men do . . . doctors in particular. You must know that."

"I?" Again, that jerk of his head. "I've had no experience in that direction. Melusine was the only one."

That, I couldn't swallow. He hadn't Tobin's good looks or Tobin's innate charm, but he had a magnificent physique . . . and some girls went for that fiery red hair. Some girls liked powerful looking 'brutes'. Perhaps, it was unfair to catalogue him as 'a brute'. There was this suggestion of leashed violence about him, but he was obviously capable of pity and a certain rough chivalry.

"Who found Melusine?" I asked abruptly.

"Reine. We were all three looking for her. My sister waded out and carried Melusine to the bank. She tried artificial respiration, while Reine ran back to the house to ring up the hospital, but it was too late."

"She called the hospital? Not Tobin or Dr Hurst Green?"

"She tried the doctors first. Dr Hurst Green was out on a case. There was no

140

reply from Badgsworth's number. That's another pointer. Badgsworth wasn't there . . . although he insists that he was."

"Hell!" I said, feeling as if I'd jarred myself against a slab of granite. "You're determined to pin this on Tobin. Why? If you didn't kill her? Afraid that your sister did?"

"Good heavens, no! Marty? That's unthinkable. She was convinced that she'd driven Melusine into drowning herself. They'd had words. They often did. Marty hadn't much patience with that poor kid. Another reason why I thought it advisable to send Melusine to The Haven." He made a rueful grimace. "Self-defence, I admit. The constant bickering got me down."

"I can imagine it. What part did Reine Elland play? Whose side did she take?"

"Reine always struggled to keep the peace." His broad forehead furrowed again. "Reine's a quiet, gentle girl. She was deeply attached to her stepmother. Unfortunately, Melusine was jealous of her. Melusine could be unkind."

"In self-defence, possibly."

"She never had any need to defend herself against Reine. The girl adored her and was perpetually making excuses for her. Reine's heart-broken now. In fact, she's making herself ill, grieving and reproaching herself . . . "

For the first time, he appeared embarrassed and hesitant. He reached for his neglected glass of sherry and drank it down as if it had been lemonade. Then, he squared his formidable shoulders and looked at me half challengingly, half in appeal.

"Miss Frodesley, will you try to understand? It's mainly on my sister's and Reine's account that I'm anxious to get all this mystery cleared up as soon as possible. I'm not just being vindictive. It's too late to help Melusine now, but we have to go on, and remorse is a heavy burden to bear."

"I know that."

"From personal experience? I wouldn't have guessed that."

"Oh, yes! I felt awful about those water-lilies . . . until I realized that it hadn't been an accident."

"Then, you should be able to sympathize with my sister and Reine. Will you come to Weirwater?"

I stared at him, bewildered. It was the very last request I could have anticipated.

"For a few days? Reine's longing to see you. She's bitter — as bitter as anyone of her nature can be — against my sister and me. She says you were the only one who tried to help Melusine, and the only one who can understand her grief."

"But . . . that's absurd. I don't know the girl."

"*Please* — " he said awkwardly, as if it wasn't a word he often used. "We're worried about Reine. We're afraid that she's heading for a nervous collapse, like Melusine's. You've had experience of such cases. You're a nurse."

"With a job. I can't suddenly down tools."

"I can fix it up with Matron. She does allow her nurses to go out on private cases sometimes. We had one for Melusine before she was transferred to The Haven. It wouldn't surprise me if Matron was glad to have you off the premises for a few days. We shall all feel the heat when the Press gets wind of developments here."

He had a point there. As I hesitated, he rammed it home.

"You would be away from it all with us. Gilburn has a man on duty at the gates.

143

Also, if you're concerned about this legacy of yours, it'll squash gossip if we're seen to be on good terms."

"Or give rise to further rumours," I said ruefully. "People will say either that I was in a conspiracy with you to eliminate Melusine or else that you're softening me up to induce me to share her money with you. However they reason, it won't look too good for you, Mr Colchard."

"D'you suppose I care a damn what people say about *me*? There was talk enough when I married Henry Elland's widow within six months of his death. I weathered it then. I can weather it again," he said roughly. "Forget about the legacy. No man would need that inducement to make a play for you — as you must know."

I stared at him incredulously.

"I don't know anything of the kind."

"Oh, don't try that mock modesty on me! I'm neither deaf nor blind," he said impatiently. "If Melusine was the type of woman who asks to be murdered, you're the type a man might do murder for — as Badgsworth may have to admit."

"I am? Oh, nonsense!"

"Yes. *You*. With those expressive eyes, that musical, beguiling voice, and that proudly aloof poise, you're a challenge and an incitement to any man with red blood in his veins. Why pretend to be unaware of it?"

He flung the words at me — in what sounded like an accusation rather than a tribute. His dark brows had drawn together and again his eyes seemed to smoulder at me.

"You're dangerous — sure enough — but I've never been warned off by the green eyes of danger," he went on grimly. "I'll take my chance. It's Reine I have to think of right now. If Matron consents, will you come to us?"

"I don't know . . . " He could be dangerous. Nobody could call him 'beguiling', but there was an odd kind of magnetism emanating from him. An animal magnetism, I told myself, trying to whip up my anger against him. "It would be rather like venturing into the lion's den — and I'm no female Daniel."

"What d'you mean by that?"

"That — whatever you feign to suspect — I believe that someone at Weirwater

145

drowned Melusine. If I were to go there, it would be because I want to know which of you did it," I answered.

"Which of us? You certainly don't lack nerve, Miss Frodesley."

9

"VERENA!" Tobin's ejaculation was startled rather than welcoming.

"I had to come. I didn't dare to ring you up — and risk being overheard," I said apologetically. "The police do listen in or tap wires don't they?"

"They would have no possible justification for tapping my telephone," he said blankly. "You could have rung up and asked me to come over to Mrs Nocton's."

"I didn't dare . . . " I said again.

"Well, since you're here, come in and have a drink!" he said, stepping back, with a travesty of his normal smile. "I don't think it was wise of you to come here so late but — "

He left the sentence dangling and ushered me into his sitting-room. He had a small flat over a block of garages, in the grounds of The Grange, Ashley Combe's one sizeable residential hotel. It was very much a bachelor's flat, sparsely and unimaginatively furnished. It suited Tobin, he had told

147

me, because it obviated any housekeeping problems. The flat did possess a miniature kitchen, but Tobin had his main meals in the hotel.

There were two other, similar flats over the garages. One was occupied by a young clerk in a local bank and the other by a retired Naval officer, a widower, who acted as secretary to the Ashley Combe Golf Club. Dr Hurst Green had plans for installing Tobin in a house in the town, with a surgery and dispensary, but Tobin wasn't enthusiastic. He didn't want to have to cope with — or pay — a housekeeper. Probably because he was the product of a large, permanently hard-up family, he disliked spending money. At The Grange, he could keep his overheads down to a minimum. The terms for permanent residents were extremely moderate.

"Well?" he asked, when he had installed me in one of the impersonal looking armchairs and had brought me a tumbler of gin, lime and soda water, in which the gin was barely evident. "What's happened? Gilburn been after you again?"

"No. Leigh Colchard."

I could have wished that Tobin had been

more generous with the gin. I was feeling somewhat battered.

"Colchard? What did he want? To induce you to hand over your legacy without legal proceedings?"

"I wonder why everyone takes it for granted that he wants Melusine's money," I said thoughtfully.

"I should have said it was obvious. Why else would a tough like Colchard have married that poor little wretch?"

"She clung . . . and he was sorry for her. He appears to conceal a soft streak behind that tough outer skin." I looked at Tobin appraisingly. "Poor little wretch? She was very pretty and appealing, Badger. Didn't you think so?"

"Darling Verena, when did I ever go for small, fair-haired, blue-eyed females? You should know my preferences by this time." His tone was deliberately light, but I fancied there was a wary look in his eyes. "What did Colchard do or say to send you rushing to me for support?"

"That's not the idea at all. Support, I mean."

"Still madly independent? Looking the whole world in the face and not fearing any man? How provoking you can be, my love!"

"It's quite a while since you've called me that. It may have been appropriate once. It isn't now," I said flatly.

"Isn't it? In whose opinion? If I elect to love you, how d'you propose to stop me?"

He was giving me the old treatment ... the affectionately teasing tone ... the caressing glance ... the flashing smile. Why? To use me as a smoke-screen?

"Colchard thinks that there was something between you and his wife," I said bluntly.

His start was obviously genuine. He splashed some of his drink on to his jacket. With a muffled ejaculation, he got out his handkerchief and dabbed at the damp spot.

"Rubbish!" he said — but he didn't look at me.

"His theory is that she was clinging to you, limpet fashion, and that you had to prise her off you. Partly to avoid a scandal. Partly to avoid getting your lines tangled," I said, watching him.

"Of all the tall stories! I hope you told him he was talking through his hat."

"I tried to, but he wouldn't buy it."

"Hell's bells!" he said, still dabbing at his jacket. "You shouldn't spring such horrors on me. Does this stuff stain?"

"I shouldn't think so. I've never spilt any."

"Oh, no? You wouldn't, my perfectly controlled Ice Maiden! I'd like to meet the fellow who could get under your skin and rattle you."

'You already have,' I thought, but I didn't say it. 'Two of them . . . Messrs Gilburn and Colchard.'

Tobin swallowed the remains of the drink in his glass and rose to refill it. This time, he was considerably more generous with the gin, I noticed.

"Hell's bells!" he said again. "If Colchard's got this crazy notion into his head, it looks as if that wretched woman is going to give more trouble dead than alive."

I flinched at that. Even allowing for his exasperation, it sounded unpleasantly callous.

"To you?" I challenged him. "Did she cling to you?"

He paused just too long before he answered grudgingly: "She tried. It was part

151

of her disturbed condition. Compensating. Because she had this idea that her husband wanted to get shot of her."

"Curiously enough, I don't believe he did. He felt responsible for her. He kept on referring to her as 'that poor kid'. I think that was how he saw her."

"Some 'kid!' Thirty, wasn't she?"

"Emotionally, she was nearer thirteen . . . as Colchard appears to have realized. The eternal small girl, searching vainly for her errant father . . . "

"Stop it! You'll have me in tears," he said ironically. "The poor lost child. Little Orphan Annie."

"Steady, Badger! She's dead."

"So? Don't go all sentimental on me. Let's get at the facts. What grounds has Colchard for his assumptions?"

"You should know. Apparently, you were out when the Colchards found Melusine in the water."

"On my way back from drowning her? Rubbish! I did drive around for a while after I left you, but I was in the dining-room at eight o'clock, for the usual cold Sunday supper, and in this flat for the remainder of the evening."

"Reine Elland says she rang you up and you didn't answer."

"She was probably too agitated to dial the right number. Why would she ring me, anyway? Her stepmother was dead."

"How d'you know?"

"What? That the woman was dead? I was told that she had been dead for at least an hour when they found her." He was sitting on the arm of one of the small, hard armchairs, sipping his drink and tapping impatiently on the floor with one slippered foot. "What is all this, Verena? You're surely not taking Colchard's wild theories seriously? Can't you see that he's merely trying to give himself an out?"

"I don't think he is. It doesn't seem to have dawned on him that he's Suspect Number One. He's honestly mystified, but determined to get at the truth."

"He appears to have put himself across on you."

Was there a flicker of jealousy in his tone? I recalled Mrs Nocton's assertion that men could be as jealous as women.

"Nobody concerned has an alibi for that whole period. After we'd separated, you and I were both driving around until eight o'clock," I reminded him.

"That's ridiculous! I don't need an alibi. Nobody could suspect *me*. Isn't that so?"

"I don't suspect you," I said, relieved to realize that it was the truth. "You're not as impetuous as you used to be. You've learned to weigh the pros and cons. You wouldn't have taken such a risk. If Melusine had accused you of making a set at her, who would have taken her word against yours? It would have been written off as another of her delusions."

"I'm glad you appreciate that," he said ironically. "You would be underestimating your own attractions if you fancied that I would dilly-dally with any woman while you were within reach. Have I dated any other girl since you came back to me?"

I shied at that way of putting it. I had come to The Haven as a temporary refuge. I hadn't 'come back' to Tobin. He was gazing at me now with a gleam in his eyes which was equivalent to a red light.

"Careful!" I said, forcing a smile. "I shall have my head turned at this rate . . . being assured that I'm attractive by three personable bachelors . . . or four, if you count young Agrimony."

"What d'you mean? Who has been telling you that you're attractive?"

"Messrs Gilburn and Colchard."

"I like their nerve!"

"I do, too. It's a pleasant change, after being persistently down-graded by Aunt Elspeth," I said demurely.

"Now, you're trying to provoke me. You know you're *my* girl. When all this furore is over, I shall take care that everyone else knows it."

"Will you? Well, we have to weather the furore first," I reminded him hastily. "It's this Elland girl who seems to have aroused Colchard's dark suspicions of you. Could it be that you've been tampering with her youthful affections and that she feared you'd ditched her for her stepmother?"

His colour rose darkly beneath his olive skin.

"I did take her out a few times. Before you came on the scene. It was at Marty Colchard's suggestion. I couldn't very well refuse. Hurst Green and old man Colchard had been close friends. The Hurst Greens introduced me to the Colchards."

"I see. What kind of girl is she?"

"Reine? Oh, nothing special! What your

aunt would have called 'a nice girl.' A plain, gauche little thing."

"Doesn't sound like your form," I said doubtfully, puzzled by a certain reservation in his manner.

"I told you, I only took her around to please Marty. Then — " He gave me a boyish, rueful grin. "Well, you know how it works. She became too keen . . . so I sheered off her. I was sorry for her. She hasn't much of a life of her own. But . . . I couldn't let her get ideas into her head, could I?"

"Not unless you shared them," I conceded — and eyed him severely. "Why are you wriggling like that? You're keeping something from me, Badger. Better make a clean breast of it."

"It never came to anything. She's completely wrapped up in the Nurseries and that precious brother of hers," he answered with patent reluctance. "I never even got around to kissing her good night. But . . . there was a time when I was intrigued."

"Are you talking about Martina Colchard?" I asked incredulously. "Goodness!"

"What's so odd about it? There's a lot

to that girl," he said defensively. "I might have gone for her quite hard — but her only reaction was to push me on to Reine."

I shook my head helplessly. That rangy, horse-faced woman, with her deplorable lack of dress sense and her crisp, practical manner? What on earth had Tobin, with his trail of conquests behind him, found 'intriguing' about her? That she'd been immune from his celebrated charm and had had no time for him?

"It was over before it started, so you needn't hold it against me," he said irritably. "I'm not her type. I don't earn my living by the sweat of my brow and I don't know the first thing about grafting roses."

"Why should you?" I said absently. "Blast! We have got ourselves involved, haven't we?"

"Hell, no! We're not involved at all, except with each other. Let me give you another drink."

He put down his empty glass and came to retrieve mine. Then, somehow, he was on the arm of my chair . . . and his hands were reaching out for *me*, not for my glass.

"Tobin, no — " I said weakly.

"Damn it, I'm only human! I can't look at you, sitting here so coolly detached, without being tantalized beyond endurance . . . "

The caressing touch of his hands, the pressure of his lips on mine, even the smoothness of his olive skin and the silkiness of his near-black hair were dear and familiar. I was swept back into the past in a matter of seconds. How could I fail to respond to the memories which crowded in on me?

Only . . . I wasn't twenty-one now. That wild, impassioned throb of my pulses was missing. It was delightful to be held and kissed warmly and possessively by Tobin, but it wasn't the soul-stirring event that it had been. He was of my world. We knew and understood and admired each other. It seemed natural to let him kiss me . . . nothing more. My senses weren't spinning and I was in no danger of losing my head . . . as once I would have been. When one slim, practised hand began to unfasten the buttons of my shirt-blouse, I grasped it firmly by the wrist.

"Enough is enough," I told him.

"It's not enough for me," he said huskily. "Have a heart, my love! I've been starving for you for four years . . . "

"Don't exaggerate! You've managed nicely, I don't doubt."

"I never got you out of my blood. You're not going to elude me again. Don't play the coy young virgin! You're a big girl now," he jerked out, wrenching his wrist free. "You can't tell me that there haven't been other fellows . . . "

I didn't know whether to be annoyed or flattered by that erroneous assumption.

"No opportunity. No inclination," I said briefly.

"You were waiting for me? All that time! Verena . . . . "

"No!" I said firmly. "Perhaps I am an Ice Maiden or under-sexed or something, but — no, Tobin! I am not going to be ravished here and now just to gratify your masculine vanity."

"That's all you know! I've waited years for this . . . "

"Famous last words . . . or saved by the bell," I said, pricking up my ears.

"What?"

"It seems to have escaped your notice, but there's someone at the door."

"Hell!" He jerked away from me violently

as the door-bell pealed again. "I didn't hear it . . . yes . . . there is someone. Well, whoever it is can just trickle away again."

"I wouldn't advise that, because my car is parked in the drive, and it's easily recognizable," I said, refastening my shirt buttons. "Think of my reputation — if not of your own!"

He gave me a far from lover-like look . . . and the bell rang for the third time. With swift, much too practised gestures, he was straightening his tie, smoothing his hair, and passing his handkerchief over his lips. Nobody, I thought appraisingly, was going to catch Dr Tobin Badgsworth in a compromising situation, dishevelled, and with lipstick on his mouth.

I opened my handbag, found a tissue, and, with the aid of the pocket mirror removed one or two tell-tale smears from my chin. I just had time to run a powder-puff over my flushed skin. Then, Tobin was opening the door.

"Good evening, Dr Badgsworth! I hope I haven't called at an inconvenient moment?"

It was Gilburn's voice — at its blandest — implying that its owner knew exactly why this was 'an inconvenient moment'.

Inconvenient for Tobin . . . but not for *me*.

I could have embraced that slender, dandified figure, except that I had an impulse to slap the faint, significant smile from his thin lips as Tobin ushered him in and he acknowledged my presence with a graceful bow.

"Hello, again!" I said, with a lift of my chin. "Don't you ever go off duty, Inspector? Or is this one of your unofficial visits?"

"The name's Gilburn," he reminded me smoothly. "Officially, I am off duty and on my way home. There were just one or two points which I hoped Dr Badgsworth could clarify for me."

"How's that? Are they too obscure for your police surgeon? Then, consult my senior partner. Dr Hurst Green has more experience than I've yet amassed," Tobin said unsmilingly.

"No doubt," Gilburn agreed, unruffled. "Only, Dr Hurst Green is scarcely a personal friend of Miss Reine Elland's, as, I'm informed, you are — or have been."

Tobin glanced swiftly at me . . . which was, I thought, a mistake on his part.

His tone was all wrong, too; much too

elaborately casual as he answered: "Reine Elland? I know her, but I wouldn't call her a personal friend."

"No? She's young and probably over-impressionable. We're not, I may say in confidence, attaching any great weight to her statements," Gilburn said with irritating reassurance. "Don't let me drive you away, Miss Frodesley — " as I was hauling myself to my feet. "No need to break up your evening."

"Thank you, but it's getting late. And, as I've never met Miss Elland, I can't help in the clarifying process," I retorted.

"I believe you might at that. I'm not among those who scoff at feminine intuition," he said. "Why, in your opinion, would Miss Elland insist that her step-mother committed suicide?"

"I wouldn't know. What reason does she give?"

"That her stepmother had fallen in love with our friend here, and that Colchard was refusing to give her a divorce."

Tobin said: "Rubbish!" but Gilburn was looking at me.

"The girl must possess a lively imagination," I said, as coolly as I could. "Melusine

Colchard didn't give me any indication that she wanted a divorce — or that she was romantically interested in Dr Badgsworth."

"Possibly, she feared your reaction," Gilburn hinted.

"Possibly," I conceded. "I might have laughed — and she couldn't bear not to be taken seriously."

"You would have been amused?" He raised his eyebrows quizzically.

"No. Not really. I should have been sorry for her."

There was something in this man, Gilburn, which drew the truth out of me, as if by a magnet. I found it difficult to parry or evade his thrusts. Yet, though my instinct was to be completely honest with him, I had to consider Tobin. Whether I still loved Tobin or not, he had been my first, and, to date, my only love. He must be able to count on my loyalty now.

There were bonds between Tobin and me which weren't to be snapped by any outsider. Not only emotional bonds, or the bonds of friendship, either. We were dedicated to the same profession. The doctor-nurse relationship was something which was probably beyond a policeman's comprehension. A nurse always had to stand by a doctor. That was a kind of unwritten law.

I said with forced coolness: "It's not unusual for a woman patient in a disturbed condition to fancy herself in love with her doctor. All I can tell you is that Melusine Colchard did not betray any of the usual signs. She was inclined to resent both Dr Badgsworth and his partner. She imagined that they were in a conspiracy with her family. She had got it into her head that her family wanted to have her certified."

"So that they could obtain a power of attorney and handle her money?" Gilburn asked — and I fancied that he was mentally pricking up his ears. "Was that a possibility?"

"Not even a remote possibility," Tobin intervened impatiently. "Sheer delusion. Part of her persecution mania."

"She had a rooted sense of insecurity, dating back to her childhood. That's another reason why she wouldn't have attached herself to Dr Badgsworth. He's too young to represent the father figure for whom she was yearning," I contributed. "You're wasting your time, trying to pin anything on Doctor Badgsworth."

"Possibly, but Doctor Badgsworth hasn't been entirely frank with us." Gilburn turned pointedly to Tobin. "You omitted to inform us that you were in South Tapwick on Sunday evening. You must barely have missed Miss Frodesley, who stopped there for petrol just before the garage closed at seven-thirty."

I didn't think I had started — but Tobin's start was clearly perceptible. He glanced at me, frowning.

"You were in South Tapwick, Verena? Why?"

"I didn't know where I was. I was just driving around."

Again, there was a wary look in his eyes. Did he imagine that I had been following him, checking up on him?

"Quite a coincidence," Gilburn said pleasantly. "That you were both in South Tapwick . . . unknown to each other."

"A very odd coincidence," Tobin said curtly.

"Very odd," Gilburn agreed. "According to Miss Colchard's statement, she was getting over a stile into the lane, with her basketful of blackberries, when she saw your car coming from the direction of Weirwater. You drew up and asked if you could give her a lift. She thinks it must have been just after seven."

"Yes," Tobin admitted. "Somewhere around seven. I was in the dining-room here by eight o'clock."

"Miss Colchard was on her way back to the house to get supper. She refused your offer of a lift, but you had a few minutes' conversation? On the subject of her sister-in-law?"

"Principally, yes."

Tobin took out his cigarette case and offered it to me. I was aware of his tension as if it had been my own. I took a cigarette and he held his lighter to it. His hand wasn't quite steady. I touched it briefly with my own. It was the only gesture of reassurance I could offer him. He stepped back quickly, as if my fingers had scorched his. He lit his own cigarette clumsily, scorching the paper. I longed to ask him what he was so het up about — and to warn him that Gilburn's trained eyes wouldn't miss the signs of tension.

"Would you care to enlarge upon that discussion, Dr Badgsworth?" Gilburn

166

pressed him ruthlessly.

"It was confidential."

"Yes? Miss Colchard has already volunteered her version." Gilburn produced that hateful shiny black notebook and ostensibly consulted it. "In her own words, she asked you; 'Why did you let Melusine come back here? She's driving us all up the wall. I think she's crazy. For heaven's sake, take her back to that nursing-home before I throttle her.' Correct?"

Tobin was drawing hard on his cigarette.

"Something like that," he said, with obvious reluctance. "I don't remember her exact words, but she was a bit exasperated."

"More than 'a bit', surely, if she could talk of throttling her sister-in-law?"

"That was just an empty phrase. In any case, Melusine Colchard wasn't throttled . . . and she must have been already dead when Marty got back to the house."

"Odd that Miss Colchard didn't see her — or the overturned boat," I said involuntarily.

"Miss Colchard states that she didn't walk up the main drive, past the lake. She took the lower drive, which leads to the Nurseries. She found her brother there, watering rose bushes. The hose had sprung a leak, and soaked his dungarees."

"A plausible excuse — if he had just thrown his wife into the lake. I suppose that has occurred to you, Inspector?" Tobin countered.

"Naturally. A little obvious, though. He could have changed into dry trousers," Gilburn said meditatively. "A lot hinges on the last conversation he had with his wife. Unfortunately, we have only his version. Miss Colchard had gone off in a temper, and Miss Elland had retired to the bathroom to wash her hair."

"So . . . you're suspecting Marty — Miss Colchard — now?" Tobin challenged him. "That's ridiculous! She wouldn't be capable of drowning anyone."

"Would you apply the same reasoning to Miss Frodesley?"

Tobin hesitated, just perceptibly, before he came out with a firm: "Of course. She's a nurse."

"And so, presumably, hardened to death? Informative," Gilburn said smoothly. "Evidently, you consider Miss Frodesley a tougher character than Miss Colchard."

Tobin cast a harassed look at me.

"I didn't say that," he said stiffly. "Miss Frodesley has a great deal of courage and fortitude and pertinacity. I don't know if Miss Colchard has ever been tested for those qualities. What's my opinion worth, anyway? Surely, your job is to deal with facts, not suppositions? To my mind, it's clear that the husband had the best motive and opportunity."

"If he's telling the truth, he knew that his wife had already made a new Will . . . so what would he have to gain? There was no other woman in his life."

"*If?*" Tobin echoed sceptically. "Wouldn't any normal husband have tried to make things up with his wife instead of walking off and leaving her?"

Gilburn shrugged his slender, elegantly clad shoulders and consulted his notebook again.

"Miss Colchard also stated that she reproached you for not having 'looked us up lately,' and added that 'poor Reine's feeling neglected. She's heard rumours that you've been seen around with this nurse Melusine is so sold on. True or false?' To which you replied: 'Nurse Frodesley is an old friend . . . and a stranger here. There's nothing in that.' Correct?"

"More or less. Hell's bells!" Tobin said irritably. "Is it necessary to go into all these trivial details?"

"Miss Colchard appears to have been very frank with you," I said, wondering why Martina had given him such a full account.

"That's the kind of girl she is. Frank and ingenuous. It would never have occurred to her that the Inspector was trying to catch her out. She's incapable of prevarication. If she had drowned her sister-in-law, she would have admitted it," Tobin said with conviction. "I'll swear Marty had no hand in it."

"She and Miss Elland stick to it that Mrs Colchard must have committed suicide," Gilburn said dispassionately. " 'While the balance of her mind was disturbed,' Mr Colchard doesn't agree with them. Nor, I gather, does Miss Frodesley?"

He glanced inquiringly at me. Reluctantly, I shook my head. That solution would be the easiest way out for everyone concerned, but it stuck in my throat.

"It's possible, in a sudden fit of desperation," Tobin said, as if snatching at a life-line. "The childish attitude of: 'I'll make them sorry they were all so horrid to me.' It would have been simple for the husband to have clasped her hand round some water-lilies in the hope of avoiding a verdict of suicide — and the assumption that he'd driven her to it."

"Then, he should have the common-sense to admit it," Gilburn said severely. "As it is, they all deny making that gesture to convention."

"I doubt if his brain would work that way," I said. "He's not subtle. It looks like a woman's bright idea."

"You told me that you didn't know Leigh Colchard, Miss Frodesley — " Gilburn took me up swiftly.

"I met him for the first time at the lecture last night. This evening, he called to see me at the cottage."

"About the Will? He hasn't lost much time," Gilburn commented.

"No. It wasn't about the Will," I said curtly.

"Then — ?"

"I'm sorry, Inspector Gilburn, but, unlike Miss Colchard, I'm not in the habit of repeating private conversations," I flashed.

"As you've already observed, I'm neither frank nor ingenuous. Now, if you'll excuse me, I must get home to bed. I have to be on duty at eight o'clock tomorrow morning."

I headed for the door with all the dignity that my tiresome ankle would permit. Both men sprang to open the door for me. Gilburn managed to get there first. Our eyes met — and I knew from the gleam in his that he hadn't finished with me yet.

"I can't compel you to answer questions, Miss Frodesley . . . but I shall be calling on you again before long," he said . . . as if I needed to be told that!

"Drop in any time," I responded with deliberate flippancy. "There's nothing to prevent you from trying your luck."

10

WEIRWATER! It was even more beautiful in its entirety than in those slides I had seen at Martina's lecture. I couldn't drive on to the house. I had to stop. I had to get out of the car and walk over the smooth turf to the water's edge.

Weirwater! I was drawn to it as if by a magnet. I suppose one can fall in love with a place, as well as with a person. It had never happened to me before, but I had felt the first symptoms stirring in me when I had gazed at those slides. Odd, really, because I had expected to be repelled by the lake where Melusine had died. She had always spoken of it with distaste. She had found the trees 'gloomy', and the silence 'oppressive'.

Yet, to me, Weirwater had a beauty right out of this world. There was a kind of hush over it, but not silence; not the silence of death and desolation. The lake was tranquil, but it was alive. There was life on, in, and all around it. Here and there, ripples showed on the surface, where fish moved under it, or leapt up after a fly. Faintly, I could hear water splashing down the weir, through the open sluice gates. I could hear the soft rustle of rushes, too, as the light breeze stirred them.

There were no yellow irises flowering now, but I could see their sturdy clumps of sword-like green leaves, close to the water's edge. Near where I was standing, there were tall rushes, their feathery plumes waving in the breeze. Silvery leaved willows grew to one side, stretching out their branches lovingly towards the water — as if they were drawn to it, as I was. On the far side, the lake was more heavily treed. One could fancy that the wood, which screened Weirwater from the lane, was marching down to the water to drink.

There weren't as many water-lilies now as there had been in Martina's slides, but the few that were flowering had a delicate, unearthly loveliness as they raised their heads above their broad, shiny green leaves. Again, I thought how incongruous violence, or indeed any violent emotion, was in such a setting. Surely, only a singularly insensitive character, unsusceptible to beauty, could have profaned this serenity?

It could be, that having it perpetually before their eyes, the Colchards and Reine Elland had grown indifferent to it. Yet . . . could one own such a place and not love it? In due course, perhaps, I should discover the answer. That, I supposed, was why I was here. I was a free agent. I needn't have yielded to the pressures applied to me.

The pressures had taken varying forms. Leigh Colchard's had been undisguisedly an appeal for help . . . when he had rung me up to repeat his invitation.

I had answered defensively: "You imagine I can do something for Melusine's step-daughter? I very much doubt it. And . . . what about your sister? After her lecture, she stated publicly that she had 'no desire to make my acquaintance.' Are you asking me to force it on her?"

"Marty's apt to jump to conclusions. She imagined that you'd been encouraging Melusine in her delusions about me, and about my attitude towards her. I've convinced Marty that she was wrong," he had said impatiently.

"How — and why?" I had asked.

"After our talk the other evening, it was clear to me that you weren't that kind of person ... the misguided or trouble-making female who encourages a wife to think the worst of her husband. I would say that you're fair-minded and unprejudiced."

I was feminine enough to have been gratified by that tribute ... but a warning bell had been ringing at the back of my mind. Wasn't I involved enough already? Why should I let myself be drawn deeper into the Colchards affairs? That could be dangerous. I couldn't have reasoned why. I just felt the instinct for self-preservation raising its hackles.

I hadn't given Leigh a straight 'yes' or 'no'. I had tried to put Matron off, too, when she had raised the question.

"It might be a wise move, Nurse," she had counselled me. "To demonstrate that you're on friendly terms with the Colchards may squash some of the inevitable rumours. Also, it's better to negotiate than to incur the unpleasantness and expenses of a court case. One can hardly expect Mrs Colchard's family to let you walk off with all her money."

She evidently believed that Leigh's urgent invitation was aimed at taking some of my legacy off me. It was a logical assumption. I wondered why I had this conviction that he wasn't interested in Melusine's money; that his concern was primarily for Melusine's stepdaughter.

Tobin shared Matron's opinion.

"I don't like the idea of you at that confounded, eerie place," he had said, "but you're well able to take care of yourself, aren't you? It'll mean that you're off the scene when the Press gets its teeth into the case. You needn't hesitate to accept the Colchards' hospitality. It's far from disinterested."

"It hasn't been hospitality that they've offered. They — or rather he — have asked me to see what I can do for Reine Elland," I had pointed out. "What do you think of her condition?"

For a moment, he had looked embarrassed.

"I haven't seen her since her step-mother's death. Hurst Green and I decided that it would be more prudent for him to attend her. She has this idea in her head that I was involved with that wretched woman," he had answered.

It had been Dr Hurst Green who had turned the scales. He had come to The Haven on purpose to talk to me. I liked what I had seen of him and his handling of our disabled and disturbed patients. There was a basic kindliness in the man and an apparently inexhaustible store of patience. He had a vague, absentminded manner, but his pale blue eyes didn't miss much.

He had said: "I'm worried about Miss Elland, Nurse. Her step-mother's death has been a shattering shock . . . and she's all at sea, emotionally. She feels that she has no claim on the Colchards now . . . no right to stay on at Weirwater."

"I suppose she hasn't, as far as that goes," I had said, "but Mr Colchard appears to feel responsible for her."

"Yes. The poor child hasn't anyone else, even remotely related to her. It's a difficult situation. It's possible that you may be able to resolve it . . . "

"How?" I had demanded.

"You were her step-mother's friend and confidante. She may talk to you. She's holding Miss Colchard responsible for Mrs Colchard's death — and refusing to have anything to do with her. She has shut herself up in her room, in a dangerously emotional condition. We don't want her to become withdrawn."

"Why should she? She isn't Melusine Colchard's daughter, so there can't be inherited tendencies," I had protested.

"Self-induced, possibly. It's an impressionable age, and she was greatly attached to her step-mother."

"I can't help doubting that. If Melusine had felt that she really mattered to her step-daughter — or to anyone else — she wouldn't have been so desperately unhappy," I had said. "Melusine talked as if Reine Elland had a long cherished grievance against her . . . on account of Reine's father's death."

"Another of Mrs Colchard's delusions, I would think." He had given me one of his kindly, abstracted smiles. "I should be grateful if you would go to Weirwater for a few days, Nurse. You possess that rare, happy knack of gaining a patient's confidence. Happy for the patient, that is. Not for yourself. Appeals for sympathy and understanding can be wearying."

"Yes," I had agreed feelingly. "And, honestly, I'm not feeling sympathetic towards Reine Elland — or the Colchards. They all failed Melusine . . . and one of them killed her. But . . . if you want me to, I'll try to do what I can."

"Thank you! I appreciate that, Nurse. I don't believe that the police have any grounds for their suspicion that Mrs Colchard was deliberately drowned. It seems much more probable that she drowned herself in a sudden fit of despondency," he had retorted in mild reproof.

Mrs Nocton, that thriller addict, remained convinced that Melusine's death was the result of 'foul play'. She had been excited, if alarmed, by the idea that I was to visit Weirwater.

"It'll be as I said," she had prophesied. "The police'll never solve the mystery — but *you* will. It wasn't a man's crime and so men can't be expected to get to the bottom of it. Only, you'll have to be careful, Nurse dear. When you get too warm, someone may have a go at *you*. That's how it usually happens. It's the second attempt that gives the guilty one away."

"In stories, yes, but nobody has any motive for attacking me," I had assured her.

"Don't count on that. Someone may fancy that you know more than you do," she had warned me. "Besides, as I said from the beginning, jealousy's at the root of that poor little thing's death — and anyone might well be jealous of you. Look at the way the men come after you! Even that odd policeman. Don't be rash, dear, and go to meet someone in a dark, lonely place. It always annoys me when heroines do that and land themselves in mortal peril just because they can't use their common-sense."

"Not to worry, Mrs Nocton! I'm no heroine — and I'd never stick my neck out for the hell of it," I had answered.

Yet, as I stood beside the lake, I had an uneasy feeling that I had stuck my neck out by coming here. Mrs Nocton could have been right when she had said that 'the guilty one' might imagine that I knew more than I did. Nobody could be certain how much Melusine had told me. I wasn't, for that matter. I had thought her fears and suspicions exaggerated and distorted. Half of what she had said hadn't really registered on me.

"So . . . your courage didn't fail you . . . "

For such a large man, Leigh moved lightly. I hadn't been aware of his approach. I swung round, defensively.

"Did you think it would?" I countered.

"No, but I felt immensely relieved when I heard your car."

I looked at him consideringly. From his soil-stained dungarees and soil-stained hands, he had been working in the Nurseries.

"You heard my car? From the Nurseries? Yet . . . you didn't hear a car that evening? You didn't hear Melusine's cries?"

"I didn't. Want to make something of it? Care to call me a liar?" he demanded.

I shook my head.

"I haven't that amount of courage, and I don't think you would lie. Not to save your own skin, anyway."

"Thanks for the concession!" He jerked up his head in the gesture which already seemed familiar to me. "I certainly wouldn't lie to protect the handsome young doctor."

"To protect your sister, you might," I hinted.

"Marty would never need that kind of protection," he said arrogantly.

"And the girl, Reine? What precisely is

your relationship with her, Mr Colchard?"

"Relationship? There isn't any. I'm not even her legal guardian. She's nearly twenty-one. If she chooses to leave, I can't stop her." His broad forehead creased. "Can't you drop the 'Mr'? Or are you determined to stand on your dignity? Am I expected to address you as 'Nurse'? I would prefer 'Verena'. It's a delightfully uncommon name. Appropriate, too. Something to do with 'truth', isn't it?"

"I believe it means 'true picture.' It was my grandmother's name. You can use it if you wish," I said hurriedly, turning away from his scrutiny to gaze at the lake again. "I'd like to arrive at a true picture of what happened here that Sunday evening . . . "

"D'you think I wouldn't? You heard that the inquest was adjourned again?"

"Yes. Rather odd. It's as if Gilburn still isn't one hundred per cent certain that Melusine was murdered."

"You are, though. Aren't you?" he challenged me.

"So are you, it would seem."

"Yes. Mainly on account of that point you just raised. No screams. I've good hearing, and I ought to have heard

183

something . . . unless her head was held down, under the water."

I shuddered, and he said: "Not a very pleasant picture. It suggests an inhuman ruthlessness. You were looking very intently at the lake when I spotted you. Commanding it to give up its secrets?"

"No. I was entranced by the beauty of it, and thinking that nobody who loved it could have defiled it with violence."

"I said you were perceptive. For your information, that reasoning automatically rules out my sister."

"And you?"

"I?" Again, I sensed rather than saw that characteristic jerk of his fiery head. "It strikes me as ridiculous that anyone should suspect me of killing that poor kid. Confound it all, she was my wife! I was feeling guilty and remorseful enough about her as it was. Why should I have added to that burden?"

If Martina was 'frank and ingenuous', as Tobin had insisted, her brother appeared to share those qualities. I had a conviction that he honestly couldn't appreciate that in most people's eyes he would be Suspect Number One. In Gilburn's eyes, he wasn't,

I remembered. It would seem that Gilburn saw Leigh as I did.

"I believe you," I said. "It wouldn't have occurred to you to drop the said burden into your lake."

"Naturally not. I had hoped that, if Melusine was well enough to come home for the week-end, she was well enough to look ahead. In my admittedly clumsy fashion, I had been threshing around for a possible solution to our problems. Unhappily, the solution I came up with was anything but acceptable to her."

"What solution was that? Divorce?"

"Heavens, no! That would have been a defeatist answer — and no solution at all. I was responsible for her. I couldn't say 'let's call it a day', and turn her adrift."

"Then — what?"

"I don't know why I should submit to your probing into these personal matters."

"You invited it by bringing me here," I reminded him. "You must have realized that I didn't want to involve myself."

"*Touché!*" he admitted. "I asked for it — and I can see that I'm going to get it. Perhaps this is the way Melusine would have wanted it. You understood how her mind worked. I failed lamentably. I thought it was the loss of the baby which had thrown her. My suggestion was that we should adopt a child."

"Oh!" I caught my breath sharply. "That was certainly optimistic and forward looking . . . "

"It was the future that mattered. It always is. One can't undo the past, but one can build for the future."

"Melusine was bogged down in her past. She was convinced that she had failed all along the line. She couldn't have faced the responsibility of adopting a child," I said.

"So I realized, belatedly. She took my suggestion very much amiss. Unhappily, it confirmed her rooted conviction that I was yearning for a son and blaming her for losing ours," he said ruefully. "She asked bitterly if she hadn't suffered enough already from another woman's child . . . and launched into one of her diatribes against Reine. I told you about that."

"Yes. And that brings us back to the official reason for my presence here. I'd better get along to my patient."

"Right! I'll take you to her."

We turned and walked to my car. I was grateful that he didn't offer me his arm. Nor did he attempt to take the wheel. He merely opened the door of the driver's seat for me.

When he had swung himself in beside me, he said: "Now you know what a clumsy fool I am, you may understand why I can't do anything for Reine. I've tried . . . "

"Is she in love with you?"

"With me?" He started like a shying horse. "Heaven forbid! Of course she isn't. I'm right out of her age group. I'm thirty-four. According to Marty, Reine took a fancy to your doctor friend — but nothing came of it. That's not surprising."

"Isn't it? Doctors have to walk warily, of course, especially where their patients are concerned," I said defensively. "From what I can gather, Tobin Badgsworth took Reine out at your sister's prompting; not because he was attracted."

"What man could be, with you on his horizon? Are you engaged to Badgsworth — as Gilburn appears to suspect?"

"No. I'm not."

"Will you be, when all this is over?"

"Who's asking personal questions now?" I countered.

"Sorry! I just wondered . . . "

"As you observed, one can't undo the past — and it's foolish to live in it. Tobin and I might have married — four years ago — but we didn't."

"Why not?"

"Prudence prevailed," I said demurely.

"Prudence? Any fellow who could let prudence prevail where you were concerned, must need a psychiatrist or a blood transfusion. In Badgsworth's shoes, I would have grabbed you by your chestnut hair and dragged you into my cave," he said scornfully. "If that's the kind of character he is, you're well rid of him. What has prudence to do with the way you can make a man feel?"

"That sounds ominous! Are you warning me that I'm quickening your heart-beats?" I said with forced flippancy.

"As if you didn't know it! For the record, it started the moment I set eyes on you. And you don't have to make grimaces at my lack of finer feelings. I've told you that I don't give two damns for convention — "

"Hold your fire, please!" I said, when I

could get in a word. "When you let drive like that, I feel as though you're directing a machine-gun at me. You really are a most extraordinary man, Mr Colchard."

"Don't 'Mister' me, or I shall press the trigger again. What's extraordinary about being honest?"

"Your brand of honesty is quite out of the ordinary . . . Leigh. I'm beginning to see why it shook Melusine. She simply couldn't believe that you meant exactly what you said."

"Why the hell should I say what I don't mean?"

"Most people do. On account of the conventions you despise."

"You said you believed me. Are you going back on that, Verena?"

He sounded hurt. I had a ridiculous impulse to take one hand off the wheel and put it into his — as I would have stroked down Leo's ruffled fur. In some ways, this giant of a man was curiously vulnerable.

"No," I said. "But, for all our sakes, I think you'd better apply the safety catch . . . if you have one."

"Your own is obviously highly efficient."

"A nurse's has to be. And I'm here as a nurse; remember?"

"*Touché!*" he said again, resignedly. "I'll try to behave myself . . . but it'll be tough going. I've been thirty-four years waiting for this — only I didn't know it. I thought it was just a fairy-tale. I never guessed that it could happen . . . like an arrow through the heart, or a fever in the blood."

"It sounds most uncomfortable."

"It is," he said grimly. "At the same time, it's an experience I'm glad I haven't missed. What about you?"

"Poor marksmanship on the archer's part. To date, the arrows have merely grazed me."

I was deliberately keeping my tone light but I had spoken the truth. What I had felt for Tobin had been a warm affection and admiration. A girl's first taste of love could end in a deep, sometimes sweet, sometimes bitter draught. Aunt Elspeth had induced me to relinquish the glass before the contents had got into my blood. As I had told Leigh, prudence had prevailed.

Possibly, that had been due to the cautious streak in Tobin rather than in me. It wasn't easy to get the picture clear, four years later. I had a sudden conviction, though, that had my first romance been with this fiery-haired giant, I shouldn't have escaped. He would have held the glass to my lips and forced me to swallow the contents.

11

"DRIVE round to the back, if you don't mind," Leigh said. "We don't use the front door or the state rooms much."

I had been about to turn to the right, towards the impressive-looking flight of steps which led up to a stone portico. Instead, I swung the car to the left.

"We?" I echoed. " 'We' means you and your sister?"

"We've been together all our lives, except when we were away at school," he said, on a defensive note. "It's easier for Marty if we have our main meals in the kitchen. We used the dining-room, of course, when Melusine was here."

That hadn't been what I'd had in mind. I had wondered if he and Melusine had ever been 'we'. I refrained from putting the question directly to him. I had asked too many pertinent questions already. I had no justification for probing into his marriage. He might not perceive that I was trying desperately to reconstruct the 'true picture.'

"This is a large house. Quite a mansion. Haven't you any domestic help?" I asked, instead.

"Just a woman, three days a week, to tackle the cleaning. Marty does the cooking. Reine lends a hand with the chores."

"Your sister must work hard."

"She does. She's our head book-keeper, though I have a lad in the office. Marty's training him."

Was it by her own wish that Martina was so heavily involved here? That she had had no time for Tobin or presumably for any other man? Did her world revolve entirely around her brother and the Nurseries? Then, it was perhaps natural that she should have resented Leigh's marriage . . . and Melusine.

"She's older than you are," I said, thinking aloud. "Did you lose your mother when you were very young?"

"Marty has never mothered me — if that's what you have in mind. She's two years my junior. It was my father who died when we were in our 'teens. We had to turn to and keep the Nurseries going.

We've been partners," he answered, his forehead creasing. "My mother was with us until five years ago. Marty was looking after her. She had arteriosclerosis."

"That must have been tough."

He didn't answer except by a twist of his lips. I felt ashamed because he had obviously read my thoughts; that he and his sister had been allies against the world at large . . . and against Melusine.

"Leave the car here. I'll put it away for you," Leigh said abruptly, as I turned into a walled, paved courtyard.

Even the back of this house was impressive, I noted, as I slid awkwardly out from behind the wheel. The back door was of massive oak like the door of a church. It swung open and Martina came out, her tall, rangy figure clad in navy-blue dungarees and a navy-blue shirt. She marched up to me, holding out her hand.

"Hello! Glad you could come," she said crisply. "First, I have to apologize. I was terribly rude to you the other night."

"Think nothing of it," I retorted, as she seized my hand in a firm, hard shake.

"Oh, but I do! It was awful of me. My only excuse is that I was on edge . . . with all that crowd gaping at us. And, from what Reine had said, I'd got it into my head that you'd encouraged Melusine in her wild fantasies."

"I didn't — but I can't prove it."

"Leigh says you couldn't have," she said — as if that clinched it.

"A nurse hears so many confidences, particularly in a nursing-home, where one can give patients individual attention, that one doesn't always listen attentively," I said slowly. "I wish now that I had taken Melusine's fears seriously, but I thought they were inspired by her condition."

"You saw her as a mental case?" she asked bluntly.

"She had that ghastly sense of insecurity, and the hysterectomy intensified it. I had known other women who were terribly depressed after that particular operation," I said, trying to choose the right words. "There was nothing wrong with her brain. It was her emotions which had gone haywire."

Martina's forehead creased in a fashion reminiscent of her brother's.

"You blamed us for that?" she demanded.

"The main trouble went much further

back — right into her childhood and her childish adoration of her father."

"That sounds like all that psycho-analysis rubbish . . . prenatal influences and buried memories."

"I know singularly little about psycho-analysis," I answered guardedly. "My nursing experience has been of the practical kind. I didn't attempt to dig into Melusine's past. She just flung chunks of it at me, and I put them together."

"Heaven knows how you found the time or the patience! Except that — " She bit the sentence off short and glanced swiftly at her brother. "I've made tea. You'd better have a cup, Leigh, before you go back to work."

Leigh had retrieved my suitcase. He was standing beside me. Glancing at him, I detected a half wry, half amused expression in his eyes.

"Feeling in need of moral support?" he asked his sister. "I warned you not to take blunt instruments to Verena Frodesley. You'll never cow or coerce her into saying what you want to hear."

Martina flushed like a schoolgirl and turned awkwardly.

"Sorry! Come in, Nurse!" she said over her shoulder.

"I've no objection to plain speaking — if that's what you mean by 'blunt instruments'," I informed Leigh as we followed Martina into the house. "Obviously, your sister was about to remark that I listened to Melusine because I believed that it would be worth my while. It doesn't happen to be true. It was my job to try to coax her out of that brooding withdrawal. If I'd done it more efficiently, she might not have died. To that extent, I'm guilty. Not about the money."

Martina gave an incredulous little snort, but I went on steadily: "I would like to get that straight. I'd never heard of Henry Elland, except as Melusine's first husband. If I'd known that he'd been wealthy, I would have supposed that she had only a life interest in his money."

"Martina should have been christened 'Martha'. As Chancellor of the Exchequer, she is 'troubled about many things'. You'll have to make allowances," Leigh said calmly.

"*You* don't worry about money?" I countered.

"Why should I? What is money? What can it do for you? Oil the wheels is all . . . and it didn't do much of that for Melusine," he retorted impatiently.

"You may find it difficult to believe, Nurse, but my brother is a creative artist. He leaves the practical side of the business to me, while he concentrates on producing new and better roses," Martina interposed sharply.

I should have been accustomed to being called 'Nurse', but I was reminded of the Inspector's tacit rebuke: 'The name is Gilburn.' Martina seemed bent on making it clear that I was here in my professional capacity.

"Sit down, Verena!" Leigh said abruptly, with emphasis on my christian name. "Stop barking, Marty! If you don't mend your manners, the girl will have every justification for walking out on us."

"It's something new for you to worry about manners," Martina countered.

"Could be . . . but Verena is rather special . . . and the opposition is formidable. If I don't pull my socks up, how can I compete with our young doctor, or that suave policeman?"

Martina gave one of her shying horse-like starts and turned bewildered, questioning eyes on him. Leigh grinned.

"I always prefer to turn my cards face upwards," he informed me. "Am I shocking you, Verena? You'll have to get used to it. What do you think?"

"I think that you have an irrepressible, if sometimes tactless, sense of humour," I answered sedately. "You should have realized that Melusine hadn't any. At least, not of an adult form. She was amused in the way a child is — "

"What way would that be?" he asked with interest.

"On one occasion, a spoilt, temperamental patient was complaining that she couldn't eat tapioca. Sister Fulbech was insisting that it was 'good for her', and the old nursery phrase made the patient revert to the nursery. She threw her tapioca at Sister. That was the first time I heard Melusine giggle."

"Custard-pie humour? I get you!" Leigh said appreciatively. "Melusine once threw a glass of barley water at Reine, vowing that it was poisoned."

"Oh? And was it?" I inquired. "Or

didn't you trouble to have the remains analysed?"

Brother and sister both gave me the same startled, outraged look. Then, Leigh grinned again.

"That was a neat riposte," he conceded.

"As if such an idea would have entered our heads!" Martina said indignantly. "Reine was devoted to her step-mother. The incident reduced her to tears, poor child!"

"So you consoled her and mopped up the mess, ignoring the cause of it? Yet . . . it could have been true," I said, vaguely recalling Melusine's mention of the said incident. "If you two are as truthful as you would have me believe, Reine Elland must be a pretty accomplished liar."

Martina was in the act of handing me a cup of tea. Her hand jerked — and the tea slopped into the saucer.

"Sorry," she said, and turned to empty the saucer into the slop-basin. "What gave you that false impression, Nurse? It was Melusine who fabricated things. Never Reine."

"Isn't that a case of 'giving a dog a bad name'? Even if she did exaggerate, Melusine couldn't always have been lying.

I don't think she did ever consciously lie to me."

"It would be a brave — or rash — person who would," Leigh said quizzically. "Try one of Marty's scones."

"Thank you!"

The large kitchen had been partially divided. We were seated at a small, formica-topped table at one end of it. The formica was a pale blue, and the four small, modern, leather-seated, steel-framed chairs matched it. His chair was scarcely large enough for Leigh. I was acutely conscious of him, beside me. I was aware of the freckles and the pale reddish hair on his lean, tanned arms, of his squarish, tough-looking hands, of the rip in one shirt sleeve, and of the tang of earth and tobacco which seemed to cling to him. There was a dried rose leaf caught in his thick, over-long hair. I had to check myself firmly from reaching out to remove it. I had a most uncharacteristic desire to touch his hair — as I would have stroked a cat or a dog.

I wondered if he was equally conscious of me. I fancied that he was. When, inadvertently, one of his leather boots came in contact with one of my court shoes, he flinched — as if it had been his own ankle which had been jarred.

"Sorry!" he jerked out. "Not much room under this silly little table. Why do we still use it, Marty?"

"It was Melusine's idea," Martina reminded him. "Reine would be hurt if we went back to the old oak table. She's upset enough already. We have to go carefully with her."

"Why?" I asked directly.

Martina's brows drew together.

"Because we can't risk another suicide," she answered with equal directness. "That's why you're here, Nurse. To look after Reine and see that she doesn't do anything rash."

"I wasn't warned that the girl was feeling suicidal," I said, irritated by her tone. "*Another* suicide? But . . . your sister-in-law didn't drown herself."

"Of course she did. It was typical of Melusine — and typical of her to do it here. She didn't have the least consideration for anyone," Martina said tartly.

"How much consideration did you show her?" I countered — and she glowered at me.

"What do you know about it, Nurse? You've no idea how much we all had to put up with from that little misery. All right — " as Leigh made an expressive gesture. "So she's dead. It doesn't alter my opinion of her . . . "

"This is a waste of time," I said, putting down my empty cup. "If I'm here to look after Reine Elland, hadn't you better take me to her, Miss Colchard?"

"She locked herself into her bedroom and won't open the door. She hasn't had any lunch," Martina said flatly. "I hoped that, when she heard your car, she would come down . . . "

"Stop fretting about her! Leave her to Verena," Leigh said, rising. He eased his big frame out from behind the small table and paused to give me a light pat on the shoulder. "Carry on, Nurse! If you need help, open a window and yell."

"Would you hear? You didn't hear Melusine."

There was a brief, pregnant silence.

Then, he said: "No. I didn't. Because she didn't scream. Not to worry. I should hear *you* . . . "

There was a significant emphasis on

that '*you*'. Martina glanced at him. I felt a sudden pounding of my pulses.

He turned and walked out. The silence he left behind him was like a heavy, blanketing cloud. I let it hover. I was too disturbed by my own emotions to worry about Martina's.

She said at last, in an angry, accusing voice: "You imagine that my brother drowned his wife? That appears to be the general opinion. Nobody realizes how much he took from her. I wouldn't have blamed him if he had turned on her, but I know damn' well that he didn't. He's not as tough as he looks."

When roused, she had that same way of firing words at one in rapid jerks.

"I am beginning to realize that," I said, but she went on swiftly: "Now, it's starting all over again with Reine . . . tears and moods and clamouring for attention. The pity of it is that he didn't marry Reine in the first place. It's too late now. Melusine would always be between them. Oh, it's such a mess!"

I was disconcerted by her assumption that there could have been an attraction between Reine and Leigh.

I said: "The girl would have been rather out of your brother's age group."

"What does age matter? Reine was more adult at seventeen than Melusine was at twenty-seven."

"She's not behaving in an adult fashion now."

"She's putting on this hurt child act in imitation of Melusine. Because she knows Leigh can't brace himself against tears and reproaches. He grabbed you as a kind of shield . . . because he was desperate. He must have seen that he was about to be dragged down into another emotional quagmire."

"He won't be — if I can help it. I don't think you need feel so protective over him. He isn't the eternal small boy type. He just has an out-sized sense of responsibility."

"Is that surprising? First, he had poor Mother on his hands, clinging to him. Then, Melusine. Now, it's Reine." She paused, breathing hard, and looked at me, her face flushed, her eyes clouded with bewildered resentment. "Reine's a sweet girl, but — "

"Take me to her," I said briefly.

"She wanted you to come. I can't imagine

why," Martina said bluntly. "If it hadn't been for you, she might have been engaged to Dr Badgsworth now."

"That's sheer wishful thinking on your part."

"Very sure of yourself, aren't you?"

"Not at all. Dr Badgsworth wasn't interested in Reine or in Melusine. *You* were the attraction," I countered.

"I was?" Again, she gave her impersonation of a shying horse. "Oh, nonsense! Whatever gave you that idea?"

"He did. Apparently, you snubbed him thoroughly . . . "

Her colour deepened. She looked at me in a puzzled fashion.

"What else could I do? I've had so much on my hands."

"Isn't it time you began to live your own life?" I suggested. "Since you believe in plain speaking, you shouldn't resent my telling you that you're making a mistake in getting yourself bogged down here."

"I was needed."

"By your mother, no doubt."

"Melusine was nearly as helpless," she said defensively.

"She might not have been, had you left her to cope."

"Weirwater is my home. I wasn't going to be driven out of it by that miserable little creature. Not while my brother needed me." She drew herself up with a gauche dignity which was oddly touching. "If you think I or my brother drowned Melusine, I'm surprised that you had the nerve to come here."

"Nobody has any motive for drowning me," I retorted, unaware that the statement might have been listed under 'famous last words.' "How about taking some tea up to my patient?"

12

"**Y**OU can come in, Marty. The door isn't locked . . . "

The answer to Martina's tap was made in a gently reproachful tone. Martina raised her brows in a questioning glance.

"Lead on, Macduff!" I said, half amused, half exasperated by her reaction.

Delivering her lecture, she had sounded cool and capable, yet in human relationships she seemed hopelessly at sea. Hadn't it dawned on her that nobody 'played up' for long without an audience? Probably, Reine was quite as curious about me as I was about her.

With patent reluctance, Martina opened the door and stalked in, carrying the tea-tray.

"Here's Nurse Frodesley," she announced awkwardly. "Are you feeling better now? Leigh's worried about you . . . "

Entirely the wrong thing to say, I thought wryly. I could almost feel Reine smirking inwardly.

"Not now," I said calmly. "He knows I can cope."

I looked down challengingly at the girl, lying prostrate on the crumpled velvet bedspread.

"A plain little thing," Tobin, that connoisseur, had called her. Certainly, Reine Elland wasn't eye-catching but, in spite of a snub nose and too sharply pointed a chin, her face might possess a kind of elfin appeal, if she were happy and animated. At the moment, with her tousled mouse-brown hair, reddened eyelids, blotchy sallow skin, and down-drooping lips, she would have failed to attract any normal man.

"I've brought you some tea, dear. You didn't have any lunch. You must be starving," Martina said, with awkward kindness.

"You needn't have bothered. I don't want anything," Reine murmured.

"Tummy upset? We must do something about that," I said, consciously imitating Sister Fulbech's brisk manner. "Leave the tray, please, Miss Colchard! I'll see to her."

Martina gave me a startled glance, but

she put the tray down on the bedside table and headed for the door.

I continued to look down at my patient, wondering why her woebegone face didn't arouse any compassion in me; why, indeed, I had an uncharacteristic impulse to seize her by her sagging shoulders and give her a good shaking. It had never happened to me before ... this instant, irrational prejudice against a patient. It wasn't only Leigh and Martina who were worried about her, I reminded myself. Dr Hurst Green was, too.

Who was I, to set my instant reaction against his considered opinion? I supposed the answer was 'a woman.' I did possess my share of feminine intuition and perception. Both were insisting now that Reine was simply 'putting on an act.'

Well, I could 'put on an act,' too. I blessed the self-consciousness which had prompted me to arrive at Weirwater in uniform. I could 'do a Fulbech', as Harriet Wilton called it.

"I'll take your pulse and temperature ... and then I'll try if I can make you more comfortable," I said briskly, bending to take one of her outflung hands.

"I feel better already . . . now that you're here," she said in a small, low voice. "It was good of you to come. I've been longing to see you. Did you guess?"

She looked up at me with such a surprisingly sweet and beguiling smile that I blinked. It was as though someone had suddenly stamped on the brakes and then thrown my emotions into reverse gear. Had I been unreasonably prejudiced? Hadn't it been perception at all which had aroused that unfamiliar resentment in me? Had it been — shattering thought — sheer primitive feminine jealousy? Jealousy of the concern the Colchards were evincing about the girl? Jealousy mainly on Melusine's account — but also to some extent on my own?

"She told me how wonderful you had been to her. Oh, I do bless you for that! She'd had such a wretched time here. Did she tell you about it?" Reine's thin, wiry fingers fastened around mine in a feverishly intent clasp. "You weren't just humouring her? You really did care?"

"For your step-mother? Yes, I was very fond of her."

"Don't call her 'my step-mother', please.

She was like a sister to me," Reine said tremulously. "I felt awful when Leigh insisted on sending her away to that nursing-home, but I did realize that she would be safer there."

"Safer?" I echoed sharply.

"Oh, yes! Because Leigh had reached the stage when he couldn't endure the sight of her. And she, poor darling, wouldn't leave him alone. I was terrified that he would turn on her. He has a savage temper, and she didn't realize how dangerous it could be to provoke him."

She had dark grey eyes; curiously opaque. They were gazing up at me with fixed intensity, as though Reine were trying to hypnotize me into listening to her . . . and believing her version.

"You're wrong there," I said. "Melusine was afraid of her husband and of his sister."

"Is that what she told you? She would never admit it to me . . . " Reine sighed softly. "I did try to win her confidence . . . but she wouldn't believe that I was on her side."

"Why not?"

"Because of my father. We had been very

close, Daddy and I, and Melusine resented it. So silly, because he worshipped her. He thought she was an angel. It was the shock of finding out that she wasn't which killed him. Did she tell you about that?"

I shook my head and freed my hand from her clinging fingers. Reluctantly, I abandoned the 'Sister Fulbech' act. If the girl was eager to talk, I mustn't check her.

"I'm going to pour you out some tea. Sit up and drink it," I said calmly.

She jerked herself up obediently, clasping her thin hands round her bony knees. She hadn't a well-proportioned figure. Her legs were too short for her torso. Her legs and arms, revealed by her sleeveless jersey and miniskirt were skinny, but her breasts were surprisingly full, and her waist looked several inches broader than mine.

"Now, drink this while it's hot," I said, handing her a cup of tea. "Talking is thirsty work."

"It's such a relief to be able to talk. Nobody, unless it's *you*, can understand how I feel about Melusine." She took a long gulping drink of tea, as if she was indeed devoured by a raging thirst. "You may think it's strange that I should have loved her, after what she had done to my father, but she was so young and lovely . . . and he was getting old, with high blood pressure and a shaky heart."

"What did she do, specifically?"

"There was another man . . . Daddy's doctor. Oh, there wasn't anything wrong about it! He couldn't help falling for her. And, naturally, she was flattered. I begged Daddy not to let it upset him, but he was madly possessive over her. So . . . so . . . he took too many of his tablets . . . "

Her soft voice broke. Her lower lip trembled childishly. I did feel a stirring of compassion then, but it subsided abruptly when I caught the side-glance she directed at me. Confound the girl! She *was* putting on an act — and she hadn't been able to resist glancing at me to see how I was taking it.

"I suppose, if one is unhappy, it's natural to turn to a doctor," she said hesitantly. "Doctors can be very comforting. Like nurses. And Melusine wasn't herself at the time. She was terribly upset about losing her baby."

"How did she lose it?" I asked with professional interest.

She gave me an odd, defensive glance.

"Didn't she tell you? She blamed me for it. She slipped and fell. She said it was because I'd polished the floor . . . but the doctor had warned her that the baby was bound to be born at seven months. She was too small inside," she said flatly. "The baby would probably have been still-born, anyway. And she shouldn't have gone on wearing high-heeled shoes."

"I see . . . "

"Do you? She was in a terrible state afterwards. She really believed that I'd wanted her to lose the baby."

"Did you?" I asked directly.

"How could I? Daddy was longing for a son. All I wanted was for him to be happy. He was a wonderful father."

"Oh, no!" I thought wryly. "Not *you*, too. Not another father complex . . . "

"Melusine talked a lot about *her* father . . . but he couldn't have cared anything for her. He walked out on her and her mother, and never even wrote to Melusine.

Daddy wasn't like that," Reine insisted. "I wanted to go away and get a job when he married Melusine, but he wouldn't hear of it. He said he needed *me*, too. Though he adored her, Melusine wasn't anything of a companion to him. She would never go round the golf courses or go fishing with him as I did. She was a little pussy-cat; hating to get her feet wet or her hair ruffled."

That was basically true, but had Melusine been given a chance to develop an interest in her husband's hobbies? Hadn't she, perhaps, with that sense of insecurity and failure hampering her, allowed herself to be elbowed away by her step-daughter? The young could be thoughtlessly cruel and Reine, devoted to her father, might have seized every opportunity of getting him to herself.

"I had to put Daddy first," Reine said defensively — as if construing my silence as criticism. "But, honestly, I did try not to get in her hair. She was so sweet — except when she was in one of those awful, black moods. She was a bit unbalanced, wasn't she? After she lost the baby, Daddy and I tried to persuade her to consult a psychiatrist about that ghastly depression of hers, but she wouldn't. I suppose she was manic-depressive. Or do I mean schizophrenic?"

"I don't know what you mean — but neither description fitted Melusine."

"You don't think so?" Those oddly opaque grey eyes seemed to search my face. "Then, how do you account for the pattern's repeating itself? For her going half out of her mind when she lost her second baby? And then . . . throwing herself into the lake because Leigh and Martina had lost patience with her?"

"She didn't throw herself into the lake."

"She *did*. You can't believe that Leigh killed her?" she said vehemently. "I know he was furious . . . when she told him about Tobin Badgsworth . . . but he wouldn't have killed her."

"You weren't present. How do you know that they quarrelled — and why?"

"I could hear Leigh shouting and Melusine screeching at him . . ." She shuddered. "It was horrible. That was why I shut myself in the bathroom to wash and set my hair. I didn't hear what they were quarrelling about, but Melusine had told me she meant to ask Leigh for a divorce."

"More tea?" I said, and reached for her empty cup.

She gave me a reproachful look.

"You don't believe me? I suppose Tobin is denying it now?"

I shrugged my shoulders and turned to the tray to refill her cup. Certainly, someone was lying ... but who?

"Was he just playing with Melusine? Is he in love with you?" Reine asked with feverish intensity.

"Dr Badgsworth?" I met her scrutiny steadily. "You must have misunderstood Melusine — or else she was teasing you. Doctors don't 'play' with their patients. Not if they've any common-sense — and Tobin Badgsworth has plenty."

"They like to marry wealthy wives," she said, with an assumption of worldly wisdom which seemed incongruous with her dishevelled school-girl look. "Melusine had had all Daddy's money. Tobin would have found it useful."

"Much too dear at the price. To marry a woman who had been once widowed and once divorced couldn't have advanced him, professionally. Quite the contrary. He would have had to leave this neighbourhood — and that's the last thing he's anxious to do. Working with Dr Hurst Green, he's gaining valuable experience," I answered, with all the patience I could muster.

"You think you know him well . . . but does a woman ever know exactly how a man's mind works?"

"Most men are pretty transparent. Much more transparent than women. Dr Badgsworth is clever and ambitious and nobody's fool. He'd never blunder headlong into an emotional morass."

There was a pause, as if she were digesting that.

Then, she said: "You don't sound as if you're in love with him, Verena."

For some reason, her use of my christian name irritated me as much as Martina's addressing me as 'Nurse.'

"Finish your tea! Then, I'm going to wash you and tuck you up in bed," I said crisply.

"Now, you're cross . . . " Her lower lip trembled. "I didn't mean to be impertinent. It just struck me that, if you were in love, you wouldn't be able to analyse him so calmly."

"You may have something there," I conceded. "I hope I should retain a sense of values, even if I were in love, though. I'm not an impetuous, impressionable 'teenager."

She flushed, as if she imagined that I was hitting her.

"I shouldn't think you ever were," she said sulkily.

"Perhaps not. I was brought up by a maiden aunt who shrank from emotional storms as from the plague."

"You were an angel to Melusine . . . or so she said. You didn't slap her down. Why are you being unkind to me?" she asked plaintively.

"I'm not being unkind; merely practical. I want you to stop working yourself up emotionally. No point in making yourself ill."

"Nobody would care if I was ill . . . really ill," she said childishly. "I don't belong to anyone now."

"Neither do I, but I don't let it worry me," I said dryly. "I'm not a stray cat. I've no desire to be owned."

"I long to matter to someone. I'm like

Melusine. I need to be loved. I suppose it's a kind of phobia."

"You'd better ask Dr Hurst Green. I'm not a consultant."

Was I being deliberately unkind and unsympathetic? Possibly. I had responded instantly to Melusine's emotional distress. Why couldn't I respond to Reine's? Because I had sensed that Melusine's had been genuine, and that Reine's was self-induced?

I must be fair to the girl. She might be 'playing up', but she was undoubtedly in a state of nervous tension. Her pulse was irregular and her temperature was two degrees above normal. She was shivering when I undressed her and helped her into bed.

She submitted to my ministrations with a child-like docility and obediently swallowed one of the mild sedative tablets Dr Hurst Green had left for her. As I was straightening her crumpled bedspread, she clutched at my hand.

"You won't go away? You won't leave me, Verena?" she said beseechingly. "I feel wretched . . . and Marty's being horrid to me."

"Really? Miss Colchard seems most

221

concerned about you," I said, reluctantly sitting down in the chair beside her bed and allowing her to clasp my hand in hers.

"She changed towards me as soon as she knew that Melusine hadn't left me Daddy's money. I do have some money of my own — from my mother — but it's not much compared with Daddy's," she said naïvely. "Marty's bitter about Daddy's money. She thought it would be left between Leigh and me . . ."

She paused tentatively, but I refrained from comment.

"I suppose Melusine willed it to you because she was afraid Leigh might kill her for it," she went on slowly. "I'm sure he didn't . . . even though there's only Marty's word for it that he was working in the Nurseries that evening."

"His own word, too."

"Does that count? To the police? Oh, I'm so worried, Verena! Suppose they imagine that Leigh and Marty are just alibi-ing each other? I can't believe that they killed Melusine."

"Why should you believe it?"

"You don't? Oh, good! I don't, either.

Only, it's almost as dreadful to believe that she drowned herself . . . and none of us tried to stop her. Could she have been so wretched?"

"No. Try to relax now. You'll feel better if you can sleep for a while."

"I don't want to sleep. I get such ghastly dreams." She shuddered. "I keep on seeing Leigh's face — white with anger and his eyes smouldering — and hearing Melusine's crying out . . . a kind of mewling like a drowning kitten."

"Don't! You're just torturing yourself."

"He wouldn't have left her to drown, would he? He would have killed her first. When Marty's cat had kittens, he killed them. He didn't drown them," she said feverishly.

Her eyes had a heavy, clouded look now, as if the sedative was taking effect. Her wiry fingers felt unpleasantly clammy on mine. She was speaking in sudden, breathless jerks. I gazed down at her uneasily. I was beginning to realize why Dr Hurst Green had insisted that she needed a nurse. There was something morbid about the way her mind worked; something unhealthy.

"Why couldn't it have been an accident?

I don't understand why the police said it wasn't," she went on, staring at me in an unfocused fashion. "Melusine's dead. Why can't they let her rest in peace?"

"Perhaps they would have done — if you hadn't put those lilies into her hand," I said, with a flash of insight.

She gave a kind of choking gasp.

"How did you know? I didn't tell you . . . "

"You were the only person present who would have thought of it," I answered with conviction. "Why did you?"

"I was frightened. I thought Leigh had killed her . . . or goaded her into drowning herself. I thought, if she was clutching the lilies, everyone would believe that she'd overbalanced while she was picking them for you."

"For *me*? You wanted me to feel responsible? You had it in for me, because she had been singing my praises?"

"Oh, no, *no*! I was glad . . . terribly glad . . . that she'd found a friend," Reine insisted vehemently. "I was thinking of Leigh. I didn't want him to be blamed . . . "

"You didn't — then — but you do now? Is that it?"

"I'm all confused . . . " She moved her head restively on the pillow. "He's been so odd since it happened. I'm afraid of him. I've this awful feeling that he imagines I saw what happened. You won't let him hurt me, will you, Verena? Or Marty, either? She'd kill anyone who testified against Leigh."

I felt as though a sudden chilly wind was blowing right through me, numbing the blood in my veins.

"If you didn't see anything, what have you to fear?" I said, my lips suddenly stiff. "Were you looking out of a window, Reine? Did you see something?"

"I'll never tell. Never — never — *never*! Please make him believe that, Verena. Please . . . please . . . "

13

I CURSED myself for having given
Reine that sedative tablet. Before I
could get anything more out of her,
she had fallen fast asleep, as if she were
utterly exhausted.

It was a relief when those thin, clammy
fingers relinquished their feverish clasp of
my hand. I stared down at her sallow,
slightly flushed face, still conscious of
that prevailing chilliness in my veins.
Asleep, with those strange eyes closed,
Reine looked younger and more appealing.
The snub nose and pointed chin were,
somehow, rather touching. Nose and lips
twitched every now and then, like a
sleeping puppy's.

If she had been having restless, disturbed
nights, she might sleep for hours now.
When she woke, the moment of truth — if
that was what it had been — would have
passed.

"I'll never tell . . . " she had vowed
. . . and she had meant it. She hadn't

just been trying to tantalise me. She had been almost asleep. She had spoken as if the words had been jerked up from her sub-conscious; as if she felt that her only safety lay in silence.

"I'll never tell — " What? What was there which she dared not reveal? What could she have seen — or heard?

I got up stiffly and limped to the windows. They looked out on to the paved courtyard. Reine couldn't have glimpsed the lake from this room. I glanced around it appraisingly. It had scarcely registered on me till now. My attention had been concentrated on its occupant.

It was a large but sombre room, with heavy, old-fashioned mahogany furniture, and a good but uninspired carpet, patterned in browns and fawns. The curtains and the chair covers were of a heavy brown and gold brocade. The only really feminine touch was in the pink velvet bedspread. That, I felt convinced, had been chosen by Melusine. Melusine had loved pastel shades of pink and blue and mauve.

Why had Reine made no attempt to brighten her bedroom? Did she like this sombre background? It almost amounted to protective colouring. There were shadings in the carpet which matched her mouse-brown hair.

It was a surprisingly tidy room. Girls of Reine's age were rarely noted for their neatness. It puzzled and vaguely disturbed me that there were no clothes, books, cosmetics or personal possessions strewn around haphazardly. The dressing-table was bare, except for a tortoiseshell brush set. The shelf over the built-in washbasin held only the essentials — tooth brush, tooth paste, sponge and face flannel. There were no photographs on the chest of drawers or the mantelpiece. There was nothing here to offer any clues to Reine's personality . . . unless the very absence of any normal feminine clutter indicated a peculiarly secretive nature.

On an impulse, I opened the door of the large, mahogany wardrobe. The contents hung neatly on coathangers . . . brown raincoat, camelhair overcoat . . . tweed suit . . . brown pleated skirt . . . fawn crimplene suit, and a few cotton frocks. Dull, useful clothes, bought off the peg, from the look of them.

Later, perhaps, I would examine her

drawers. Now, I wanted to escape from this sombre room and my sleeping patient. I wasn't unduly sensitive to atmospheres. What nurse could afford to be? But . . . there was something here which I didn't like; something oppressive and disturbing. I had a feeling that all the pent-up emotions in Reine had been allowed to express themselves only within the confines of this room.

Leaving the door ajar, so that I would hear her if she should wake and call me, I went out on to the landing. The door facing Reine's across the landing stood open and I saw that my suitcase had been placed inside, against the wall, I walked into the room — and could have gasped at the contrast. This room faced out across the lake and the evening sunshine was streaming into it. The furniture was of the same solid, old-fashioned kind, but dark oak instead of mahogany. That was the only resemblance to Reine's room.

Whoever had decorated this other bedroom had an inborn flair for colour. Walls and ceiling were a soft, clear golden yellow. The furnishings were in what I thought of as 'sunset' colours — a riot of warm salmon pinks and golds leading into fiery flame, with touches of deep olive green. Someone in this *ménage* obviously knew how to blend colours . . .

Perhaps the key lay in the olive green. Not 'sunset', but 'roses', I had seen roses the petals of which had exactly this warm, subtle blending of shades. Not Melusine's taste. I couldn't imagine Melusine ever having experimented with flame and olive green. Leigh, Martina had said, was 'a creative artist.' This must be Leigh's handiwork.

There was an oddly unused air about the room. The colourful furnishings might have been newly acquired. There was an electric blanket in the double bed, but no other sign, apart from my suitcase, that it had been designed to be occupied.

There was a light tap on the open door, and Martina stalked in, carrying a cut glass vase full of roses . . . roses the hues of which blended to perfection with the room.

"Sorry! I forgot these. Leigh picked them for you," Martina announced, putting the vase down on the dressing-table. "It was his idea to give you this room . . . "

"It's a beautiful room," I said appreciatively. "Did he choose this uncommon colour scheme?"

"Yes. How did you guess?" she asked naïvely. "He had it done over for Melusine, before they were married. It was one of those surprises which misfired. She didn't like the colours and she wouldn't sleep facing the lake."

"I wonder Reine didn't beg for it," I said.

"Reine doesn't go for gay colours. Anyway, Leigh wouldn't have wanted her to have it . . ." She checked herself abruptly. After a pause, she said briefly: "There's a bathroom next door. You won't mind sharing it with Reine? How is she? When I glanced in just now, she was asleep."

"Yes. She'll probably sleep for hours." It was my turn to hesitate. "She certainly has something on her mind," I added warily. "Something which, she vows, she'll never tell. She hinted that it concerned your brother."

"I don't believe it . . ."

With that, she swung round and marched out of the room.

I crossed to the dressing-table and buried

my face in the fragrant, velvety petalled roses. They were beautifully arranged. Could a man who cared deeply for roses and was sensitive to their subtle colourings be capable of violence?

Why not? Why was I determined to believe in Leigh? Was it from intuition? Or was it because I was drawn to him, stimulated by him, and excited by the interest he was evincing in me? I couldn't deny that, when he was close to me, I felt anything but an 'Ice Maiden.' Leigh had the strongest possible motive for 'softening me up,' hadn't he? Why, then, should I be stubbornly convinced of his sincerity? From sheer feminine vanity? Surely not. Thanks to Aunt Elspeth, I had considerably less than the normal share of that commodity.

It might, of course, be reaction against my aunt and her training which was attracting me to Leigh. Perhaps I had a secret yearning for a man who despised conventions, didn't hesitate to speak his mind, and could be 'a bit of a brute.' To be seized and kissed by Leigh Colchard wouldn't be 'pleasant,' but a shattering experience. With a sense of shame, I admitted that if that experience should come my way, I wouldn't try to elude it.

Bracing myself, I went into the bathroom. It was a delightful bathroom, with tiled walls in palest aquamarine and a peach coloured bath and washbasin. The window was of frosted glass but, when I opened it, I had quite a good view of the lake . . . and of the stone paved terrace above it. From this vantage point, Reine could have overheard a heated exchange on the terrace. She could have seen a boat on the lake. The drive was visible, too. She could have seen a car . . .

Even if it had been parked under the trees, Tobin's white Rover could have been glimpsed from here. I clutched at the sill. Had it then, come to this, that I was ready to throw my first love to the wolves, if that would keep them away from Leigh?

I hadn't known that it could be like this . . . that loyalty, affection, prudence and common-sense could be swept away like twigs over the weir, in one fierce surge of a stronger, deeper emotion.

A car was turning into the drive. I recognized it with a feeling akin to panic; Gilburn's expensive car with Gilburn at the wheel. He was as persistent as any hound. Whose trail was he following here? Leigh's? Martina's? Mine?

I drew back from the window, shuddering. Perhaps I had never fully realized before how ruthless and relentless the forces of the law could be. Certainly, I had never previously had any reason to fear or shrink from the police. I had always been on the right side of law and order. Now . . . ? Was I still eager that Gilburn should arrive at 'the true picture?'

I went back to the lovely sunset and rose hued bedroom. I stood by the dressing-table, automatically applying powder and lipstick, with the scent of Leigh's roses poignantly sweet in my nostrils. I straightened my cap and smoothed down my apron.

It seemed a long time . . . and yet all too short . . . before Martina came upstairs to call me.

"That policeman's here again," she said. "He wants you."

"Yes. I know . . . "

Why on earth had I said that? The answer seemed to have been jerked up from my sub-conscious. But . . . incredible

234

though I would have thought it a week ago, I knew now that it was true. I could no longer joke about 'the three personable bachelors' who were 'trying to turn my head.' Those three men did want me . . . for varied reasons. Again, for varied reasons, I might have responded to any one of the three.

Inspector Gilburn had come formally to the front door. He was waiting in the large, sombre hall, shadowed and gloomy, with a dank air of disuse. His slender, elegantly garbed figure was barely visible in the fading light. I felt myself shuddering again as he stepped forward to greet me.

"Hello! Another few words?" I said, with brittle flippancy.

"If you please . . . "

"That's an empty phrase," I said accusingly. "It wouldn't be any use saying that it didn't please me to talk to you."

"I hope it isn't all that much of an ordeal . . . "

I had, as once before, a feeling that I had hurt him; hurt the man, not the policeman.

"It's dark and dank here. Let's go out on to the terrace," I said — and he moved swiftly to open the massive door.

In silence, we walked down the flight of steps. He made as if to take my arm but I contrived to elude the gesture. I felt rather than saw the tightening of his lips.

There were seats on the terrace of rustic wood. I sank down on one, wondering if Melusine had sat on it for that last exchange with Leigh. If, indeed, it had been the last . . .

Gilburn sat down, facing me. Where Leigh had sat? Oh, no! Leigh wouldn't have been sitting. He would have been striding up and down, restively.

"There are times when my job is far from easy. Do you have to make it harder for me?" Gilburn asked abruptly.

"I don't want to . . . but don't you see? We're on different sides of the fence," I answered wryly. "You're hunting . . . "

"You're no hare, Miss Frodesley."

"Hare — or fox — or tiger — it makes precious little difference. Hunting simply doesn't appeal to me. It's like rat catching. Rats have to be kept down, but the process is not in my line," I said, willing him to understand. "I'm a nurse. My job is to help to heal people. Not to hound them. There's nothing personal about it. I recognize that you have to go ahead . . . but I can't go along with you."

"Right now, I'm not hunting. I came here to see you . . . to beg you to go back to The Haven," he said, in a tone oddly devoid of expression. "I called there this afternoon and was disturbed to learn that you had come here."

"I'm sorry about that . . . "

It wasn't an empty phrase. I was sorry about a number of things concerning this man, Gilburn. In his cool, ultra civilized fashion, he had been the first man for years who had penetrated my defences. There was an odd kinship between us and our sense of values. I could easily have grown accustomed to Gilburn and his deliberately under-stated personality.

But . . . in our professional lives we diverged too sharply and irrevocably. It would be futile to form any attachment to a man who was a delightful companion only in off duty hours. "Once a policeman . . . once a nurse . . . " As he had observed, we never really were off duty. Too much of ourselves was involved in our working lives.

"It's natural, I suppose," he said, as if reading my thoughts. "My job is a handicap at times. People are repelled by it, even though they concede that it's necessary."

"It isn't that, exactly. I admire you for doing it, fairly and efficiently," I said slowly. "But . . ."

"*But*? Oh, yes! *But* . . . you're more in sympathy with a doctor's, even to the extent of letting yourself be landed here." He shook his head at me. "Not very wise to act as a shield for Dr Badgsworth. Shields can be penetrated."

"It was Dr Hurst Green who induced me to come here. To look after Miss Elland," I said defensively.

To my annoyance, I felt my skin burning. Evidently, he had drawn his own conclusions from my presence in Tobin's flat the other evening.

"Is that so? What do you make of her?"

"I haven't reached any conclusions yet . . . except that she knows more than she's prepared to reveal."

I hesitated. Then, feeling obscurely that I owed him something, I told him that Reine had been responsible for clasping the water-lilies in Melusine's hand. He didn't evince any surprise. He merely nodded gravely.

"With the impulse to protect her man? Which man, Miss Frodesley?"

"I don't know. I'm not sure that I want to know."

"That's a change of heart . . . "

"I was seeing everything from Melusine's viewpoint. I was deeply sorry for her. Now, I'm beginning to realize that it wasn't only she who suffered. She made other people suffer, too. Not deliberately, but because her own emotions were hopelessly confused. They blinded her, so that she couldn't see other people's."

"That doesn't alter the issue. Nobody had any justification for drowning her, because there is no justification for taking a life," he said inexorably. "You'll concede that?"

"Yes. Of course."

He produced a platinum cigarette case, snapped it open and offered it to me. I didn't want a cigarette, yet I couldn't appear to repulse the gesture. He lit my cigarette and his own from the lighter set into the case. The flame flickered into life at a touch. That seemed characteristic of the man. All his personal possessions were of the best possible quality. It was a subtle compliment that he should, however remotely, have thought of adding *me* to them. Only, that could never have worked. He lacked the spring which could kindle that instant flame in me. His approach was too cool and intellectual.

Perhaps he was too highly civilized and educated. It could be that I needed someone more direct and primitive, more of a savage to set me ablaze. I felt ashamed to have to admit it ... but Aunt Elspeth had trained me to face facts.

We smoked in silence for a minute or two; a silence which began to weigh heavily on me.

"Why did you come here this evening?" I asked at last.

"For reassurance, possibly. I'm up against my superior officers. Not," he added with a half smile, "an unusual state for me. To my Superintendent there is a clear cut case against the Colchards. Quite simply, he's convinced that Leigh Colchard drowned his wife to prevent her from altering her Will ... and his sister acted as his accessory."

"Oh, no! He knew that she had made a new Will."

"We have only his word for that," Gilburn reminded me dryly. "Our Chief Constable is loth to have Leigh Colchard arrested, because he knew the father rather well. He would prefer to hand the whole affair over to Scotland Yard. The Superintendent and I want to clear it up without outside assistance. Unfortunately, we can't see eye to eye on the persons involved."

"No?"

"I don't believe that this crime was committed for money."

"Neither do I," I said, with a relief I hoped he couldn't detect. "And I don't believe that Leigh is lying."

"Which brings us back to Dr Badgsworth . . . and yourself . . . " he said, eying me appraisingly. "He might have eliminated the woman to preserve his professional reputation . . . "

"She couldn't have hurt it. Who would have taken her word against his? In any case, I don't believe that she was in love with him."

"I think she was. I also think that he

241

acted from fear of losing you."

"Oh, heavens, no!" I protested, aghast. "You're on the wrong trail there. I don't mean all that much to Tobin . . . and he's too cautious to stick his neck out for any woman."

"Then, what is your theory?"

I shook my head helplessly — and again a heavy silence descended on us.

"So . . . you can't . . . or won't help me?"

He didn't speak reproachfully but I was conscious of an implied reproach.

"I'm inclined to agree with my landlady," I said impulsively. "She insists that jealousy was the motive . . . that this was a woman's crime and that only a woman will solve it."

"The said woman being yourself? You'll have to be quick about it. The hounds are becoming restive," he said dispassionately. "Jealousy? Any girl might be jealous of *you* — but of Melusine Colchard? No. I can't swallow that. Don't insult my intelligence by offering me red herrings."

"I didn't mean it that way. It's simply that I can't believe either of those two men guilty."

"It isn't in order to try to pin something

on the Colchards that you're here? You're not determined to find an out for Dr Badgsworth?" he said sceptically. "Why run this risk, then?"

"I can't see that there is any risk as far as I'm concerned. At least not of the kind you have in mind."

He gave me a long, questioning look. Then, he shrugged his shoulders and rose, in one graceful, catlike movement.

"Be careful! That's all I ask. Don't keep information to yourself . . . or sleep behind an unlocked door."

"Don't go out on the lake with anyone or leave the car in an unlocked garage," I added with a forced smile. "Thanks for the warning, but I don't intend to give you another mysterious death to investigate . . . "

I had no logical reason for fear, yet, after Gilburn had gone, I began to realize what Melusine had meant about the lake. A mist was rising from the water and, in the fast fading light, there was an eerie look about it. The breeze had dropped and the air was deathly still. The shadows under the trees seemed to darken and lengthen, stretching out over the water.

No rustling in the rushes now. No friendly chirping of birds. Only an occasional plop-plop from the lake itself as the fish rose. The mist and the silence and the dark shadows could affect a high-strung, over-imaginative woman's nerves. Even I had a queer, uneasy feeling . . . as if the water was reaching out for me, pulling me towards the weir . . .

"Nurse! Nurse!"

Martina's sudden shout shattered the unearthly hush.

"I'm here!" I called back, turning towards the house.

"Come upstairs! Quickly . . . "

Martina's voice sounded from somewhere above my head. I looked upwards and saw her. She was leaning out of the bathroom window, signalling frantically.

"I'm coming. What is it?" I called apprehensively.

"It's Reine. She's being terribly sick. She's in an awful state. She says someone has poisoned her . . . "

14

"YOU kept your head remarkably well, Nurse . . . but that was what I would have expected of you," Dr Hurst Green said approvingly. "Certainly, I'll have these samples analysed, but I don't anticipate that they will contain traces of poison."

"You don't?"

"Ask yourself, Nurse! You must have realized that the pain which was apparently devastating our patient was almost wholly psychosomatic."

"I didn't have time to stop and think but . . . yes, you could be right," I said in swift relief. "You believe she was merely reacting against the sedative?"

He shook his head.

"I doubt it. Obviously, she had taken something of an acutely irritant consistency . . . but not what is generally understood as 'poison.' A large dose of ipacacuanha or Epsom salts would have had this effect."

"Or a detergent?"

"Scarcely. There are no traces of burning in her mouth or throat." He put the two bottles I had handed him carefully away in his case and shook his head again. "Keep a close eye on her, Nurse. I'm inclined to doubt that she swallowed the tablets you gave her."

"Someone could have changed the tablets," I said uneasily.

"Why would anyone do that?" he inquired.

"Because . . . because she knows more than she's prepared to tell. About her step-mother's death," I blurted out. "Someone could have intended to frighten her into holding her tongue."

"You've been reading too many thrillers, Nurse," he said in mild reproof. "Not that I have anything against thrillers. They can be valuable, therapeutically. They release some of the buried aggression from which most people, in our so-called civilized society, suffer to some extent."

"Do we? You think there's a streak of savagery in all of us? Waiting to be released?"

"Not in the case of Miss Colchard. I

know her well. I attended her mother for years," he said — as if tacitly warning me not to jump to conclusions. "She doesn't bottle up or bury her emotions. She lets them rise to the surface and spill over — and so you're unlikely to see her at The Haven."

"That applies to her brother, too."

"Undoubtedly. Reine Elland comes into a different category. For a girl of her age, she is alarmingly repressed. Even more introverted than her step-mother was," he said reflectively. "I'm hoping that you'll act as a safety-valve, Nurse. Try to reach her. If you can't, I shall suggest that she has treatment at The Haven. She's in an extremely disturbed condition."

"The shock of her step-mother's sudden death . . . " I said hesitantly. "If she really was fond of her stepmother."

"*If?*" he echoed, and gave me one of his abstracted smiles. "Yes. There is a big '*if*'. Go on using your perception, Nurse. I'll look in again in the morning."

As I closed the door after him, Martina came striding into the large, gloomy hall.

"Well?" she demanded. "Is Reine going to be all right?"

"Yes. Not to worry."

"Not to worry? When she accused me of poisoning her?" Martina gave an outraged snort. "What am I suspected of having put into the teapot? Arsenic? Weedkiller? Slug bait?"

"I don't know. Dr Hurst Green has taken the samples to be analysed."

"It's what you think. Why else did you collect the samples? You're determined to pin something on us," she said savagely. "At any rate, Leigh is in the clear. I made the tea for Reine after he had left the kitchen. Remember?"

"Yes. You would go to considerable lengths to protect your brother, wouldn't you?"

"Is that a crime?"

"No . . . but it isn't necessary. He didn't drown Melusine. You should be ashamed of yourself for suspecting him," I said bluntly, heading for the stairs.

"You don't realize how infuriating she could be . . . "

"To *you*, no doubt. Not to him. He's a big man — in more senses than one.

He saw her as 'that poor kid.' Just one of his responsibilities, like your mother," I said. "Melusine hadn't shot any arrows into his heart."

"What on earth d'you mean?"

"That he didn't care enough to feel savagely towards her. It's like our patients at The Haven. Some of them drive their relations half round the bend, but we nurses can cope because we're not personally involved."

I left her to digest that and hurried back to my patient. Whether Reine had been feigning sleep earlier this evening or not, it was obvious now that the injection Dr Hurst Green had given her was beginning to take effect. She was lying on one side, curled up like a sleepy puppy. Her face, except for its sallow tinge, was as white as her pillow.

She half raised her heavy eyelids when I crossed to the bed. She flung out a hand in my direction.

"Verena . . . Verena, don't leave me. I feel ghastly . . . " she whimpered. "Am I going to die?"

"No. Of course not. Just relax. You'll soon be feeling better," I answered automatically.

"Why did she do it?" she asked fretfully. "I swore I'd never tell."

"You would feel better if you did tell all you know," I said tentatively. "Wouldn't it be a relief to tell *me*?"

"I daren't. You'd tell the police. That policeman was here again, wasn't he? What did he want?"

"Just to talk to me . . . "

How had she known of Gilburn's visit? Had she slipped out of bed and watched us from the bathroom window?

"I thought you'd come here to look after *me* . . . not to find things out for that man. He's in love with you."

"I can't imagine what gave you that idea . . . "

"Oh, I can sense things like that! Besides, I heard Leigh talking about him to Marty . . ."

"You've very acute hearing, Reine."

"Yes." The flicker of a smile touched her lips. "It's no use for people to try to hide things from me. Melusine never could . . . " She moved her head restively. "Melusine's dead now. She won't make any more mischief."

I looked down at her thoughtfully. Mischief making wasn't a weakness which

I would have attributed to Melusine.

"I'm sleepy . . . " Reine said, her voice slurring. "Don't leave me, Verena! Don't let anyone hurt me. I'm frightened. It's awful when people hate you."

"Nobody hates you, Reine. Try to sleep now."

"Why didn't *he* come? He's being very unkind to me. He hasn't been near me since . . . since . . . you know."

"No?"

"He sends that old man instead. Why doesn't Toby come?"

My pulses gave a lurch. I had thought she was referring to Leigh. Not Tobin . . .

"He thinks it's wiser not to call here," I said. "Safer."

"Safer? I wouldn't hurt him. I'll never tell. I won't even tell you, Verena . . . "

"You don't have to tell me anything," I said, feeling as if a cold, heavy weight was pressing on my heart. "I know. At least, I've guessed . . . "

She didn't answer. Perhaps she hadn't heard. Her eyes had closed. She was beginning to breathe deeply and evenly. I sat motionless beside her while the sombre room grew steadily darker . . . and the true picture began to take shape before my eyes.

Someone must have been talking out of turn. Graphic accounts of Melusine's death and of the police investigation were in the newspapers next morning. The more sensational papers had photographs, too. There was even a photograph of me. Some enterprising reporter must have unearthed it from the files. It had been lifted from a hospital group, enlarged and printed in the papers at the time of Aunt Elspeth's death. Quite a flattering photograph, but I could have wished now — as I had wished then — that it didn't make me look so cool and serene.

Martina and Leigh both exploded over the newspaper stories . . . and appeared naïvely surprised that I didn't.

"The story was bound to break eventually," I said. "I don't know how Gilburn has kept the reporters at bay all this time. The mysterious death of a beautiful and wealthy woman . . . two adjourned inquests . . . a widower who's a celebrated rose grower . . . and a nurse who's the beneficiary of a fantastic Will . . . What more could any newshound ask?"

"I don't know how you can take it so calmly," Martina said blankly. "Have you read what's hinted about you?"

"I don't need to read it. I can guess."

"This paper almost suggests that you were responsible for both your aunt's death and Melusine's," she said in a shocked voice. "It's positively libellous."

"Not if it's 'almost', and not quite," I reminded her.

"And they've raked up all that sticky business of Henry Elland's death. Oh, it's abominable! Leigh — " She swung round on her brother. "Can't we do something about it? Do we have to let those — those vultures get away with it?"

"What do you suggest that we should do? As Verena says, it was inevitable," Leigh answered shortly.

"But . . . but . . . why now?" she asked helplessly.

"Because there's a rumour circulating that Scotland Yard is to be called in — and that suggests a major crime," I answered — and felt the colour ebbing from my cheeks as I re-read that ominous paragraph. "Gilburn hinted at it last night. It's the

253

Chief Constable's idea."

"Hell! More badgering," Leigh said wryly. "I'm beginning to wish I'd kept my mouth shut."

"What d'you mean?" I said perplexedly.

"I started all this. Didn't Gilburn tell you? When I was trying to revive that poor kid, I noticed the mark, under her hair. Like a bruise. I didn't see how, if she'd taken a deliberate plunge into the water, she could have banged the back of her head . . . and I said so."

"Oh! Then, that's why Gilburn believes your version?" I said, light dawning. "It was lucky for you that you did call attention to the bruise. The police surgeon would certainly have noticed it. Gilburn realizes that you were honestly puzzled and not just covering up for yourself. I suppose the Superintendent imagines that you looked for it because you knew it was there."

"Is that what you think?" Martina demanded. "Hell! This is as much your doing as anyone else's, Nurse. If you hadn't encouraged that spoilt baby — "

An imperative gesture from Leigh checked her.

In the sudden silence, I said: "Melusine

254

wasn't 'a spoilt baby.' It's odd that only Leigh, apart from me, seems to have seen that. She was deprived of affection and protection at too early an age . . . and the yearning for them was a burning hunger in her. Perhaps Henry Elland satisfied that hunger but, after she'd lost their baby, things weren't the same between them . . . "

"All that psychology nonsense . . . what good did it ever do her? If she hadn't gone to The Haven — "

"She would still have altered her Will . . . and she would still have died," I said with conviction.

They both stared at me.

"Yes," I said, answering the unspoken question in their eyes. "The picture's pretty clear to me. Only, there's no proof. It's going to be difficult to get any proof. Tobin Badgsworth might be able to . . . but I doubt if I can induce him to try. Doctors have to keep their hands scrupulously clean."

Before they could ask me what I had in mind, the telephone bell pealed. Martina stalked off to answer it. Leigh got out his pipe and began to fill it. I rose to collect the breakfast things.

"Verena . . . " he said, his broad forehead creasing. "Don't take any chances. Leave things to the police."

"Scotland Yard? That'll mean that we're all put through the hoop again. Besides, this is Gilburn's case. He should have the credit for solving it."

"You've a weakness for that man. What can I do to counter it?"

"You don't have to do anything, Leigh," I said, smiling at the characteristic directness of his words and glance. "There's nothing of the hound in me. I'm always on the side of the hunted. Yes, even now . . . "

"It looks to me as if we're all being hounded."

"But . . . only one person has reason to shrink from the pack. Don't worry! This hateful publicity won't last. Gilburn will have posted a policeman to keep reporters and sightseers out of Weirwater — and we're not obliged to answer the telephone."

"What about my customers? If they can't ring up or call at the Nurseries?"

"The state of siege won't last long. Afterwards, you'll have floods of orders."

"We can use them." He lit his pipe, then

looked at me again. "You haven't seen my roses yet."

"No. I want to see them, but I would rather wait till all this is over. Water-lilies will always evoke painful memories. Let's leave the roses out of this."

"Right! Provided you promise not to rush away before you've walked among the roses with me."

"That's an easy promise," I said lightly ... but I felt my pulses pounding.

Martina came back, snorting and looking more than ever like a startled, shying horse.

"The nerve! The impertinence!" she exploded. "Would we care to make a statement to some paper or other, indeed!"

The telephone bell pealed again.

"Take the confounded receiver off and leave it off," Leigh advised her. "No point in letting yourself get rattled."

She seized the loaded tray and marched off to the sink. Leigh eased himself from behind the blue-topped table, looking harassed.

"You mustn't mind Marty," he said in a low, unfamiliarly deprecating tone.

"I don't." Once again, I had an absurd

impulse to stroke him; to gentle him with a touch. "It's all right. I can cope."

"Bless you!"

His expression lightened transparently. I could read his mind as if it were an open book. How often, in this 'breakfast nook' had he tried vainly to stand between his sister and his wife? To appease Martina and to shield Melusine? Or to counter Reine's sly digs at both of them? If he hadn't been a big man, in every sense, he must have become soured by the strain. It wasn't going to happen again; I would take care of that.

I watched him as he headed for the door. He looked so formidable, yet he was emotionally as vulnerable as a child.

"Nurse — " Martina had swung round from the sink, and was watching me.

"Yes?" I said, meeting her scrutiny and feeling a certain compassion for the bewilderment in her eyes.

"I'm sorry. I didn't mean to bark," she said awkwardly. "It's just . . . Leigh. He's such a blundering fool."

"I understand. Only, you don't have to protect him against me. I won't hurt him."

"I don't see how you can help it. He never could hide anything from me. I know what has been in his mind, ever since he saw you at the Garden Club Meeting. It isn't just gratitude because you were good to Melusine."

"I know."

"Do you? He didn't even resent your legacy. He's not a bit practical. He doesn't realize what everyone will say, if — if he chases after you. And it's so hopeless," she said in a rush. "You're going to marry Toby Badgsworth. That's why Toby cooled off poor little Reine."

"Tobin Badgsworth is a wary bird. With his looks and his charm he can't prevent girls from falling for him — but he can and does avoid getting involved with them," I said.

"He wants to get involved with you."

"Because I eluded him once . . . and he isn't accustomed to being frustrated. Also, he thinks I would make a suitable wife for an ambitious doctor. I should understand that his profession has to come first. I shouldn't make scenes or gossip . . . " Perhaps I was being unfair to Tobin, but I had to draw the picture in simple lines to make Martina see it. "I dare say Tobin and I could achieve a good working partnership; a conventionally 'happy marriage.' But . . . I've discovered recently that I'm not really calm and conventional."

"Are you going to marry Toby or aren't you?"

"I'm not. I don't want to spend the rest of my life conforming to my aunt's rules, admirable though they may be."

"You mean that Leigh stands a chance?" she said incredulously. "You're not just tantalizing him?"

I shook my head . . . and the telephone bell pealed again.

"Leave the receiver off the hook, as Leigh suggested," I said. "I must get back to my patient."

I had already washed Reine and taken her a breakfast tray. I found her in the bathroom. She turned quickly, almost guiltily, at my entrance.

"I — I'm feeling sick again," she faltered.

"Oh, no! Don't try to pull that trick on me again," I said firmly.

"Trick?" Her grey eyes widened innocently.

"You know . . . and I can guess. I've

been nursing for quite a while. Come back to bed and let me get you ready for the doctor," I said, taking her arm.

She wriggled, but she let me lead her back into the bedroom and tuck her up in bed again.

"Will it be Toby?" she asked naïvely. "I like Toby . . . "

"You've a thing about doctors," I said. "Why did you pretend that it was your step-mother who was interested in them?"

"Don't call her my step-mother," she said, in the tone of a sulky child. "She wasn't a proper wife to Daddy. It was more as if she was a pet he'd adopted."

"That was what you wanted to believe. Only, you couldn't, after you knew that Melusine was going to have his child," I said, keeping my tone calm. "That must have upset you badly. Was that why you tried to convince your father that Melusine was having an affair with the doctor?"

"You mustn't say things like that. You're here to take care of me . . . not to bully me," she protested. "I told you, I just wanted Daddy to be happy."

"Yes. With you. Not with his wife."

"It isn't true! How can you be so unkind to me?"

"Is it unkind to try to let out the poison that's festering in you? Jealousy can wreck your life as it wrecked Melusine's."

I was treading on dangerous ground; rushing in where a skilled psychiatrist might hesitate. I had nothing but intuition and perception to guide me — and both could be mistaken.

"I was never jealous of Melusine. How could I be? She was such a fool. I was sorry for her," Reine said with feverish intensity.

"She was very lovely and appealing . . . "

"She never appealed to any man for long. She was such a bore . . . She expected to be petted all the time . . . like a spoilt child. She couldn't even give Daddy his medicine . . . "

"*You* were the spoilt child, Reine — until your father married again. You always resented Melusine," I said steadily. "She's dead but you're still alive. You have a chance, if you'll take it; a chance to free yourself, by facing the truth."

She began to cry then; to accuse me of being cruel to her, and to insist that she had loved Melusine dearly.

"She loved me, too . . . and now I haven't anyone to care about me. You don't understand how I miss her," she wept.

"I'm afraid I do understand . . . only too well," I said ruefully. "When the object of any strong emotion is removed, there's a dreadful blank left. Believe me, I am sorry for you. I want to help you . . . before it's too late."

It was no use. I couldn't reach her. She went on crying till Dr Hurst Green appeared.

Then, she burst into an incoherent indictment of me and the Colchards and Tobin. We were all being unfair and unkind. Nobody cared what happened to her. She might as well be dead . . . like Melusine.

Dr Hurst Green heard her out with the kindly patience characteristic of him, until, exhausted, she relapsed into a childishly sulky silence.

"You're still suffering from shock," he pronounced. "I'm going to give you something to help you to relax."

Afterwards, when I was seeing him to the hall door, he said in mild rebuke. "Your attempts at therapy would appear to have been a shade too drastic, Nurse. You won't break down this patient's resistance with a pickaxe."

"I'm sorry, but it's a question of time. There's an urgency," I said defensively. "Reine knows what happened when Melusine was drowned. I have to get it out of her."

"For whose sake?"

I felt myself flushing, but I answered candidly: "For everyone's. Before Scotland Yard is called in to the case. Isn't it better that I should catechize Reine than that some professional detectives should? For her own sake as much as for the Colchards', she has to tell all she knows."

"A determined and inexorable young woman, aren't you? I must remind you that a nurse's first duty is to her patient."

"You don't have to remind me. It may be dangerous to attempt the kind of mental surgery for which I haven't had any training . . . but it seems to me more dangerous to let the poison penetrate any further into her bloodstream," I said. "She might kill herself next time . . . instead of making herself sick."

"You've tumbled to it that the nausea was self-induced?"

"Yes. She's craving to be in the centre of the picture. She doesn't realize that she's destroying herself. Without Melusine to concentrate on, she's all at sea . . . " I checked myself there, conscious of the knowledge behind his tolerant smile. "I'm sorry. I suppose you can see it all more clearly than I can. Only, it might take weeks of your specialized treatment to achieve a break-through — and it's pretty hellish for the other people involved in this grim affair."

"My concern is not with the other people," he reminded me. "If you can win that poor, confused child's confidence, so much the better, but go gently with her, Nurse."

"I'll try, but . . . "

"I don't want there to be any 'buts' about it. I appreciate your loyalty to my partner, but he's old enough to safeguard his own interests. If he has behaved unwisely, he'll have to foot the bill. He would be the first to admit that."

15

"WHY do you have to keep on nattering? Melusine's dead. Why can't we forget about her?" Reine asked reproachfully.

"Can you? Can anyone who was involved with her?"

"I promised I wouldn't tell. You're trying to make me break my promise. You would be sorry if I did," she warned me. "The police will never prove anything as long as I keep quiet."

"And this cloud of suspicion will hang over all of us indefinitely. It isn't good enough," I said firmly.

She pouted, and I braced myself for the next move.

"I do understand that you can't break your promise," I said. "But . . . you could show me."

"Show you? How?"

"We could act out the scene. You could pretend that I was Melusine . . . and show me what happened to her."

I held my breath, not daring to look at her. Would she take the bait? Had I made it tempting enough?

After a long pause, she said: "You wouldn't want to do it all. If you overturned the boat, you would get very wet. And you wouldn't be able to swim with that groggy ankle."

"I should have to rely on you to pull me out of the water," I said lightly. "I expect you can swim."

"Oh, yes! Daddy insisted that I learned to swim when I was quite small. He wouldn't take anyone out fishing with him who couldn't swim. He tried to teach Melusine, but she was hopeless. She was afraid of cold water . . . "

I suppressed a shudder. Should I always be haunted by my mental picture of Melusine, struggling in that deep, cold water, among those serenely lovely lilies? Perhaps she hadn't struggled, though. She hadn't screamed. There had been that bruise on her head which Leigh had noticed . . . Remembering that mark, I wondered if I was about to stick my neck out a shade too far. Perhaps I would be secretly relieved if Reine ignored the bait . . .

"We wouldn't have to overturn the boat. I could just show you where it happened . . . and how," she said.

"It might help to get the whole ghastly nightmare out of your system."

"Yes. It might." She gave me that curiously beguiling smile of hers. "We could do it this evening . . . when Marty's at the W.I. Meeting and Leigh's in the Nurseries. Then, there wouldn't be anyone to interfere."

"If it wouldn't be too much of an ordeal? I don't know anything about boats. You would have to row."

"It's just a light dinghy, with paddles. There's a punt, too, but it was the dinghy Melusine used. The punt wouldn't have overturned so easily," Reine explained.

"Can you handle it?"

"Of course. I used to row Daddy about when he went fishing. He said I was quite a professional oarsman. I could cast a fly, too. He taught me. He liked to pretend I was the son he had wanted. We had the most terrific fun together. He didn't really miss my mother at all . . ."

She went on talking about her father and I schooled myself to make the right and tactful responses. I fought down the chilly sickness which was rising in me.

I could see the 'true picture' much too vividly now ... the fond and foolish father, not realizing what he was doing to his young daughter, encouraging and enjoying her devotion till her whole world centred around him — and then pushing her into the background when he married his lovely young wife. Perhaps, in his blundering, masculine fashion, he had thought he was doing the best thing for Reine by keeping her at home and insisting that he still needed her, but it had been a terrible mistake. He should have sent her away to make a new life for herself. Probably, he had come to rely on her uncritical affection, not guessing how possessive it had become.

Heaven grant that I could love without jealousy or possessiveness! That awful, clutching desire to own another person could bring untold misery with it. Wasn't it responsible for half the 'in-laws' problems from which women like Mrs Thompkin suffered? Couldn't it goad the most easy-going of husbands to revolt and kick over the traces? Leigh had endured it, but it had left him baffled and sickened, ashamed because in the last resort his only defence had been to walk away . . .

"It's very silly of Marty to go to the W.I. this evening . . . but she is stupid, you know," Reine said, with a curious complacency, as we watched Martina's elderly Morris 1000 chugging down the drive. "She doesn't realize that everyone will be staring and gossiping."

"She has her own brand of courage. To meet trouble head-on comes naturally to her," I said.

"I don't think she's brave. She's too stupid to see what's staring her in the face. Poor old Marty! I'm sorry for her," Reine proclaimed, with an air of superiority which made me squirm inwardly. "Shall we go down to the boathouse? You'd better put on a coat, Verena. It'll be chilly."

"Not until the sun goes down . . . " I saw her frown and perceived the danger of appearing to thwart her even over a trifle. "This jersey will do."

We walked in silence down the drive and then across the grass to the small boathouse, built against the bank. My pulses were thudding. Was there a barely perceptible movement among the trees on the opposite side? I didn't dare to look . . .

"You must tell me what to do," I said, as Reine opened the boathouse door. "I'm not sure how to launch a boat."

"You don't have to try. She didn't. She just stood here, looking helpless, while the boat was held for her," Reine said patronizingly. There was a smile on her lips and a look of pleased anticipation in her eyes. "You'll have to imagine the car . . . a sleek white car . . . just down the drive. I'm not going to tell you whose car it was, or who got out of it and came to help Melusine. We'll pretend that I'm that person."

"You're good at make-believe, aren't you, Reine? It was a pity Melusine wasn't. She was inclined to see everything and everyone through dark glasses . . . including herself."

She ignored that. She was like a child, directing a playmate in a nursery game. She helped me into the dinghy and seated herself at the paddles. With swift, competent strokes, she propelled us out across the smooth, silvery water.

"Can you remember the exact place? You must have very good sight to have marked it from the bathroom window," I said, swallowing down the bitter taste in my mouth.

"Oh, yes! I have," she answered readily. "I inherited it from Daddy. He never needed reading glasses. Do you see that clump of lilies? Those were the ones she was trying to reach. You'll have to lean over, as she did. He didn't take the boat quite close enough. I think he was angry with her. I think she'd been telling him things . . . about asking Leigh for a divorce so that they could get married. Only . . . he didn't want to marry Melusine. It was just her imagination . . . "

"No," I said evenly. "Not Melusine's imagination, Reine. Your imagination. What did she say to you to make you angry? Something about me?"

"She said you were going to marry Toby . . . that everyone at that Home knew he was crazy about you . . . " She stopped abruptly, staring at me. "That was earlier. I don't really know what she said to him. I'm just guessing."

"A good try, but it isn't convincing.

You see, I know Tobin. He wouldn't have taken Melusine out on this lake," I said flatly. "She was leaning over . . . yes. What then? Did you suddenly feel that you couldn't endure the sight of her a moment longer? Did you hit out at her without knowing what you were doing?"

"Oh, no! She leaned over too far . . . and the boat tipped. I was trying to grab her . . . " Her strange eyes widened childishly. "How did you guess? I didn't mean to push her."

"Not consciously, perhaps, but subconsciously. And when she was in the water?"

"It was horrid. She was gulping and gasping . . . making noises like a drowning kitten. I was afraid Leigh might hear . . . and blame me. So . . . so . . . "

I had been watching her intently. Even so, I was unprepared for the swiftness with which she raised the paddle. I dodged the savage, descending thrust before it could land on my head . . . but it caught me a glancing blow on one shoulder. I jerked sideways too violently. Then . . . the light boat was heeling over . . . and I was in the water.

It was unpleasantly cold and clammy — but not as cold as I had anticipated. I heard Reine calling out hoarsely but I didn't surface. I swam as fast as I could under water, until my lungs seemed to be bursting.

Hoping that I had put a safe distance between myself and the boat, I came up for air . . . to find myself seized and hauled to the bank by a dripping Inspector Gilburn.

"Miss Frodesley . . . are you all right?" he panted.

"Of course. I told you I would be." I looked at him severely. "There was no need for you to spoil your expensive suit. I asked you to watch . . . and not to intervene."

"That girl meant to kill you . . . You had no business to run such a risk . . . "

"And after I've handed you your case on a platter! What ingratitude!" I cut him short. "It was the only way. She wouldn't have killed me, except by accident. She was just lashing out in a blind, childish rage. As she had lashed out at her step-mother."

I had to let him help me up the bank. It would have been churlish to have wrenched away from him. Shaking the water from my face and hair, I turned to glance back at the lake. The dinghy was floating upside down among the lilies. Two large, very wet policemen were floundering through the shallows. One of them was carrying Reine. She wasn't struggling. She had wound her arms round his neck, and was weeping quietly on his broad shoulder.

"What will happen to her?" Leigh asked, his forehead furrowing.

"I suppose she'll be charged with manslaughter — or perhaps only 'grievous bodily harm.' It wasn't premeditated. Just a boiling over of her pent-up emotions," I assured him.

"She seemed so genuinely concerned about Melusine . . . and so shocked by her death," he said in bewilderment.

"She was. She was beginning to realize that she'd lost her main *raison d'être*. For years, she had been concentrating her energies on resenting Melusine and making trouble for her. When there was no longer anyone to excite her jealousy, she felt a ghastly blank. I managed to induce her to transfer some of her frustrated emotions to me," I said. "Dr Hurst Green will probably flay me for it — but it worked. Don't worry about her, Leigh. She'll be a lot happier now than she has been for years past."

"Happier?" he echoed.

"Of course. She'll have all the limelight on her . . . the police, the Press, solicitors, doctors and psychiatrists hovering round her, making her feel that she's really important at last. She'll have herself a ball. Young Maurice Agrimony will almost certainly volunteer to defend her — and he'll probably cure her of her thing about doctors."

I met his puzzled, baffled scrutiny and smiled.

"I'm not being callous. I'm just light-headed with relief. Because, up till the very last, I couldn't be one hundred per cent certain that I was right about Reine."

"I can't imagine how you guessed. It would never have entered my head to suspect her," he said helplessly.

"I don't think Gilburn was much wiser. It was really Mrs. Nocton who gave me the answer . . . before I'd met any of you. She was certain that Reine must have been bitterly jealous of her step-mother. And

276

then . . . Reine was the only one with wet hair and a cast-iron excuse for it," I said reflectively. "Only, she overdid it when she told Gilburn that she had been trying out a new colour rinse. When I brushed her hair for her, I couldn't detect any signs of artificial colour."

"You've so much intelligence and perception that you make me feel myself a blind, clumsy fool," he said wryly.

I had changed into dry clothes, and we were sitting in the kitchen over the pot of strong, fragrant coffee which he had insisted on making for me. He got up to refill my cup — and the flimsy table rocked ominously.

I felt my skin burning. Had Gilburn resented my solving his case for him? Would Tobin think I had been 'showing off' . . . and incidentally risking my patient by an over precipitate and dramatic action? Would the aftermath of tension and suspense impel everyone concerned to turn and rend me?

"I'm sorry," I said. "I was desperate. I knew that nobody would believe me if I had only a theory to offer. I had to find proof. Are you furious with me?"

"Naturally," Leigh said grimly. "At least, you had the sense to alert Gilburn — but why did you keep your crazy plan from me?"

"Because I knew you would intervene. Gilburn's a policeman first and a man second. I knew that he would do what I said and wait behind the trees . . . "

"I wouldn't have let you run such a risk. Why did you? On Gilburn's account? Or on the doctor's?"

"If you must ask such unnecessary questions, wait till we take that promised stroll among the roses."

His grim expression lightened.

"You haven't forgotten that promise, then? That's something! How long do I have to wait?"

I was deadly tired and my ankle was throbbing, but I could no more have resisted that ingenuously hopeful, eager, vulnerable look in his eyes than I could have snatched a saucer of milk away from one of Mrs Nocton's cats.

"It's still quite early . . . " I said. "Martina won't be back from her meeting for another half hour at least. The sun's beginning to go down, but roses look beautiful at sunset and their fragrance is stronger then, in the falling dew . . . "

He didn't wait for me to finish. He was seizing me and hauling me to my feet. Unfamiliar, delicious little tremors ran through me at his touch. I let him put his arm around me and lead me out of the house. The air was warm and still. The sun was going down in a blaze of splendour.

"There'll be time to show you my newest rose . . . the rose I shall call 'Verena' . . . " he said. "And — well, quite a lot can happen in half an hour . . . "

Quite a lot did . . .

THE END

TO FIGHT THE WILD
Rod Ansell and Rachel Percy

Lost in uncharted Australian bush, Rod Ansell survived by hunting and trapping wild animals, improvising shelter and using all the bushman's skills he knew.

COROMANDEL
Pat Barr

India in the 1830s is a hot, uncomfortable place, where the East India Company still rules. Amelia and her new husband find themselves caught up in the animosities which seethe between the old order and the new.

THE SMALL PARTY
Lillian Beckwith

A frightening journey to safety begins for Ruth and her small party as their island is caught up in the dangers of armed insurrection.

IN PALE BATTALIONS
Robert Goddard

Leonora Galloway has waited all her life to learn the truth about her father, slain on the Somme before she was born, the truth about the death of her mother and the mystery of an unsolved wartime murder.

A DREAM FOR TOMORROW
Grace Goodwin

In her new position as resident nurse at Coombe Magna, Karen Stevens has to bear the emnity of the beautiful Lisa, secretary to the doctor-on-call.

AFTER EMMA
Sheila Hocken

Following the author's previous auto-biographies — EMMA & I, and EMMA & Co., she relates more of the hilarious (and sometimes despairing) antics of her guide dogs.

SKINWALKERS
Tony Hillerman

The peace of the land between the sacred mountains is shattered by three murders. Is a 'skinwalker', one who has rejected the harmony of the Navajo way, the murderer?

A PARTICULAR PLACE
Mary Hocking

How is Michael Hoath, newly arrived vicar of St. Hilary's, to meet the demands of his flock and his strained marriage? Further complications follow when he falls hopelessly in love with a married parishioner.

A MATTER OF MISCHIEF
Evelyn Hood

A saga of the weaving folk in 18th century Scotland. Physician Gavin Knox was desperately seeking a cure for the pox that ravaged the slums of Glasgow and Paisley, but his adored wife, Margaret, stood in the way.